KU-725-373

TIME ENOUGH

TIME ENOUGH

Carol Wood

CHIVERS

British Library Cataloguing in Publication Data available

This Large Print edition published by BBC Audiobooks Ltd, Bath, 2008.
Published by arrangement with the author.

U.K. Hardcover ISBN 978 1 405 64346 7
U.K. Softcover   ISBN 978 1 405 64347 4

Copyright © Carol Wood 1999

All the characters in this book have no existence outside the imagination
of the author, and have no relation whatsoever to anyone bearing the
same name or names. They are not even distantly inspired by any
individual known or unknown to the author, and all the incidents are
pure invention.

All rights reserved.

Printed and bound in Great Britain by
Antony Rowe Ltd., Chippenham, Wiltshire

3 8002 01908 5283

CAN

This book is to be returned on or before
the last date stamped below.

P.S.89740

TILE HILL

5 NOV 2010

24 DEC 2016

Caver rd|16

SE 7/17

2

5

WILLOW

11 JUN

14 JUN
9 AUG
CAN - TIL 9/13

20 SEP 2014

2 OCT 2016

F
4
15
15
5
i
17
016
6

To renew this book take it to any of
the City Libraries before
the date due for return

Coventry City Council

CHAPTER ONE

Dr Kate Ross glanced anxiously at the time on her wristwatch, then at the small clock on the car's dashboard. One-twenty. Ten minutes to go. In an hour the interview would be over. And by this evening she would finally be able to make plans for her future. Her preoccupation with time caused her to sigh.

This sigh did not go unnoticed by her friend, Angela Lawrence, who sat next to her in the driver's seat. 'You look fabulous, Kate,' Angie said encouragingly. 'Just try to relax.'

Kate smiled, though her large blue eyes were apprehensive. Not for the first time, she thought how lucky she was to have such a good friend in Angie. They had been close friends since school and had kept in touch regularly even though their ambitions had taken them in different directions.

At eighteen Angie had met and married Nick, continuing her nursing training until the birth of her son, Phillip. Kate had qualified as a doctor, remaining in south London where they'd both grown up. Angie, now a practice nurse, lived with her family in Oxfordshire. Knowing that Kate was intending to move, she'd written and told her of the vacancy for a locum at Milchester Medical Centre where she worked.

'And you say that Dr Withycombe's replacement is arriving from South Africa in the autumn?' Kate asked, as Angie drove her small blue Fiat through Milchester High Street. 'So they want a locum for approximately six months?'

Angie nodded. 'Yes, that's right. May to October or thereabouts.'

Kate was lost in thought for a moment. Two years had passed since her broken engagement, and sometimes it surprised her that she was able to think of a future now—of a life without Julian. She wasn't running away, she told herself firmly, just putting the past behind her where it belonged and starting afresh.

Milchester was the first step to her future, and she hoped she'd be successful in this interview. Full-time general practice would boost her confidence and she certainly needed that! But if she was unsuccessful in her application for the locum's post here, she'd set her sights further north—to the Dales and its beautiful, picturesque countryside.

A small frown pleated Angie's forehead. 'As I explained, Dr Buchan has interviewed a number of applicants, but he hasn't found them suitable. Don't worry, you're not seeing him today. Glyn Withycombe will be interviewing you and he's great.'

Kate sighed with relief. 'Thank goodness it's Dr Withycombe, then!'

Angie laughed. 'Oh, Dr Buchan's OK once you get to know him, but he lives for the practice—and his boys, of course.'

'Boys?' Kate frowned.

'Mmm,' murmured Angie distractedly, as she negotiated the traffic. 'Twins of thirteen. He's a widower and has virtually brought them up on his own. Some would say he's a workaholic—certainly he's dedicated to his practice and has very high standards.' Angie shrugged and changed the subject. 'Anyway, if Glyn offers you the job, Phillip's room is yours for as long as you want while you find some suitable accommodation.'

'Thanks, Angie, I appreciate that.' Kate smiled warmly. Angie's house was always full of kids. Even Angie's long-suffering husband, Nick, had been known to protest at the human density squeezed between its walls. Phillip was thirteen and his sister Miriam, nine. Kate didn't feel happy about adding to the chaos but, then, she hadn't even had the interview yet, let alone secured the job.

Kate gazed out of the window as they drove through Milchester. Once it had been regarded as a pretty market town, but over the last decade—and Kate had seen the changes herself when she'd come to visit Angie and Nick—new housing and industrial estates had sprung up and a new section of motorway had been built for the busy commuters to London.

The heart of Milchester, however, remained

old town, and the cattle market was still functional, though carbooters now replaced livestock. As Angie slowed down, Kate recognised the leafy green park that was close to their destination. A few minutes later they arrived at Angie's place of work, Milchester Medical Centre. The modern, cream brick building stood in front of a large car park which bordered the Red Lion Hotel where, quaintly, a thatched roof protruded over a vined wall.

Angie parked the car in one of the vacant spaces allotted to staff. 'You'll be fine,' she reassured Kate again as she switched off the engine. 'Don't forget, you can discuss anything with Dr Withycombe—he's the salt of the earth. You go on in. I'll gather my things together and see you in there.'

Kate nodded, took a deep breath and pushed open her door. Would Dr Glyn Withycombe prove sympathetic to her recent illness? she wondered. Some doctors were still reluctant to accept the existence of ME—the abbreviation given to myalgic encephalomyelitis, more widely known as chronic fatigue syndrome.

Once through the surgery's large glass doors, Kate nervously smoothed down her new midi-length oyster cotton skirt and soft blue silk blouse which she hoped effectively hid her weight loss, an unfortunate result of ME. Her mane of shining, honey blonde hair was drawn

4

back from her face and neatly plaited to reveal the twinkle of two, tiny pearl earrings set in the lobes of her ears.

'Got to rush, it's my Friday stop-smoking clinic!' Angie gasped breathlessly, rushing up beside her. 'You look lovely, Kate. Good luck—and don't forget to smile!'

Kate dutifully parted her lips in a brave smile. Angie hurried off to her patients and Kate was left in the centre of a large open-plan waiting room. One glance at the reception desk told her it was a typical Friday afternoon when last-minute ailments took priority before the weekend.

The desk was divided into four partitions, each one equipped with a computer. Four queues had formed at the positions, while other patients sat on brightly coloured up-holstered benches and chairs, talking among themselves or reading magazines.

Kate had just begun to count the many doors leading off Reception when someone touched her elbow. A tall, dark-haired man gazed down at her. He wore a smart grey shirt with a darker, unpretentious tie. He was clean-shaven and his silvery eyes swept over her, his frown deepening as she gazed at him blankly for a moment.

'Dr Ross?' he enquired in a deep voice.

'Dr Withycombe?' But she realised it wasn't Glyn Withycombe immediately she'd said the name—this man was mid-thirties, nowhere

5

near retiring age.

'No, I'm Dr Buchan—his partner. I'm afraid Glyn's indisposed this afternoon.' He held out his hand and Kate took it, though her heart sank as she recalled Angie's less than enthusiastic remarks about the man who was now staring down at her. 'It's Ben,' he said in a friendly enough fashion. 'And I believe it's Kate, isn't it?'

She nodded. 'Yes, it is.' She retrieved her fingers from his powerful grip and tilted her head questioningly. 'I'm sorry to hear about Dr Withycombe. Nothing serious, I hope?'

'No, not at all,' he was swift to assure her. 'Glyn's grandson sabotaged the plumbing system. Glyn and his wife are looking after their grandchildren for a week, and at lunchtime Nigel hammered a nail into one of the floorboards. Unfortunately it fractured the central heating piping beneath and there was a minor flood.'

'The joys of being a grandparent,' Kate remarked with a smile.

'Thank God I've no experience of that—yet.' He was about to continue speaking when one of the receptionists called his name from the desk. Turning to her, he raised his hand in acknowledgement. 'I shan't keep you long,' he said as he returned his attention to Kate. 'Take a seat for a minute or two.'

However, Kate was too tense to sit down. She watched him walk away, her eyes taking in the long, loose limbs and broad shoulders which comprised a very good, fit-looking body—no doubt the result of exercising thirteen-year-old twins, she thought ruefully.

Not wishing to stare, Kate looked back to the patients who filled the waiting room. She caught the glance of a woman in a red and gold sari. She smiled, was rewarded by one in return. From the other corner of the room two young students were talking in a language Kate suspected was Japanese. Sitting on another bench, several middleaged women were huddled deep in conversation, no doubt discussing the intrigues of their small group.

Kate's gaze finally went back to the desk. Dr Buchan had left it and was walking towards her.

'Shall we have a look around?' he asked as he arrived beside her. She nodded, following him through one of the doors leading from Reception. 'There are six consulting rooms, one for each member of staff,' he told her as they entered a long, carpeted corridor. 'This is Glyn's, here on the right.'

Kate gazed into a large, well-equipped room, admiring the profusion of fresh green plants and the brightly coloured beanbags placed on the floor for the benefit of the younger children.

'When Glyn and I bought this place seven years ago,' he continued as they made their way along the corridor, 'it was much too large, but luckily we'd anticipated the growth of the town. Meg James followed the next year, then Damian Stewart. Bal Chandra and Rupert Greaves are our most recent partners. They've been with us for the last eighteen months or so.'

Kate was impressed and continued to be as they walked on through the corridor and upstairs to the offices, staff-rooms and stockrooms on the first floor. Returning to Reception, Kate noted that the patients were called by tannoy to each doctor, and in addition multilingual signs were pinned to the walls in order to avoid any possibility of confusion.

Once back in Ben's consulting room, Kate occupied the patient's chair, while he sat opposite her, sliding his long legs under the desk. 'Glyn tells me you've known Angie Lawrence since your schooldays,' he began, 'and that you've worked mainly with inner-city practices. I understand a period of ill-health caused you to take some time away from work?'

Kate nodded. 'I was diagnosed with ME three years ago, just after my twenty-eighth birthday.' She added hesitantly, 'But for the two years before that I'd been experiencing bouts of fatigue . . .' She shrugged. 'In retrospect I feel they were probably due to the onset of ME.'

'It must have been very distressing for you,'

he said, and crooked an eyebrow.

'Yes, it was,' Kate answered honestly, 'especially as I'd been offered a partnership at the practice where I was working. I'd have accepted had my symptoms not worsened. I took six months' leave, but as my health deteriorated eventually I felt it was fairer to everyone to give in my notice.'

He looked at her curiously. 'And you returned to work . . . when?'

'In spring of last year. I took a part-time post as a locum for a female GP who was pregnant and needed cover for a few months.'

'But it was only part time?' he asked her keenly.

'Yes,' Kate admitted, 'although often I worked longer hours in order to cover for other members of staff who were on holiday or sick.'

There was a long pause while Dr Buchan considered this, his brow furrowed in a deep frown. Kate's heart began to sink as the atmosphere in the room seemed to grow noticeably cool. 'In other words,' he said at last, his tone clearly doubtful, 'Milchester would be your first attempt at full-time practice since the ME. Don't you think that it's rather soon to be taking on such a demanding role?'

The silence was deafening as Kate tried to conceal her bitter dismay at his attitude—not that she hadn't expected it after what Angie

9

had told her during their earlier conversation. This man quite plainly felt that she was not up to the job, and had no qualms in telling her so.

She stared into his sceptical gaze and suddenly felt it would be impossible to convince him, no matter what she said, of her determination to return to—and succeed at—full-time general practice. Forcing herself to look steadily into his eyes, she shook her head determinedly. 'I consider myself one of the lucky ones—one of the few who recover from ME within a relatively short span of time,' she answered firmly. 'I'm quite confident I'm back to full health, but I can assure you if I had any qualms at all I certainly shouldn't have thought of applying for a position here. I can see for myself the centre is a very busy practice.'

He tightened his full mouth into a straight line, his dark gaze seeming to bore straight into her. 'The workload within a fundholding practice such as this is extremely demanding. Like most commuter towns, there's a fierce need for efficient, round-the-clock health care and it goes without saying that we've a duty to provide it. I'm sure you *think* you feel well,' he continued coolly, 'and I admire your determination to return to work so swiftly, but I have to admit that I'm doubtful Milchester is what you're looking for.

And . . .' he sat back, lifting dismissive eyebrows ' . . . wouldn't it be even more unwise to jeopardise your health for a position which holds no career prospects? A colleague of mine, arriving from South Africa later this year, is replacing Glyn. We shall only require a locum until October at the latest.'

Slightly shaken at what seemed to be a polite but unequivocal dismissal, Kate forced herself to nod. 'Yes, Angie explained, but my own intention is to move away from the London area, possibly to the Dales. If anything, I feel that Milchester would be . . .' She hesitated, trying to find the right words, but before she could speak again, he cut her short.

'You thought we might prove a suitable starting point for your return to full-time employment?'

Kate could not miss the note of cold irony and she began to wish that she'd never let Angie persuade her into applying for the job. It would have been simpler to have enjoyed a brief holiday with Angie and her family, then do as she'd planned—leave the south behind and head north to the picturesque countryside of the Dales, which she'd decided would make the perfect place to renew her career.

The recollection of the few tentative and positive enquiries she had made flashed through her mind. In the light of Ben Buchan's plain disapproval, they seemed decidedly alluring. Kate decided that following up her research six months earlier than she'd anticipated would be a lot less painful than sitting here, enduring a fruitless interview which had only increased her sense of vulnerability.

She rose to her feet and held out her hand. 'Thank you for seeing me, Dr Buchan,' she said in a crisp manner, lifting her small chin.

'It's Ben,' he reminded her quietly, and looked up at her. 'Are you leaving?'

'I don't really think there's much left to say, is there?'

She was amazed to see him smile. 'Please, sit down. I'm sorry if my directness upsets you, but I think it's only fair we both know how we stand from the very start.'

'The start?' Kate repeated confusedly.

He waited for her to sit down again and when she had, folding herself uneasily into the chair, he continued. 'I'm well aware you were—are familiar with inner-city practice procedure, and I'm sure your experience more than qualifies you for Milchester. But ME is extremely debilitating, and though the vast majority of sufferers retain their motivation and want to get better and rejoin the rest of the world they don't put themselves in the firing line quite so swiftly after recovery. I just wanted to make sure we both understood that.'

'But I've had no return of *any* symptoms since Christmas!' Kate heard herself protest defensively, not at all certain whether he was offering her the job or merely debating a point

12

about ME. 'I'm sure I'm well now. At least, as sure as I possibly can be.'

His grey eyes suddenly lost their silvery glint of coolness and became thoughtful. He was silent for a moment, lifting his large hand to run it slowly over his chin. Just when Kate thought she could bear it no longer, and was about to stand up once more, he spoke. 'There is one more consideration,' he said in a voice that held her in continuing suspense, 'and that's accommodation.'

Kate stared at him blankly. Did this mean he really was considering her for the job? Quickly she tried to gather herself. 'Accommodation? Well . . .' she fumbled, 'I assume there are letting agencies in Milchester, aren't there?'

He gave an uncertain shrug. 'There is one fairly decent one. Lassiters . . .' His voice tailed off as a dark eyebrow arched. 'You might find something there, though the properties which are to let in Milchester all look as though they've seen better days. Still, I'll give you their address.' He reached out for a pen and drew a pad across his desk towards him.

Stunned, Kate took a deep breath. 'Am I to understand you're offering me the locum position?'

He looked up and tilted his dark head. 'You still want it, don't you?'

Kate was so surprised that for a moment she didn't respond, but when she'd recovered from

13

the shock she found herself nodding. 'Yes, I do.'

A faint smile played at his lips as he scribbled an address on the pad and leaned back in his chair. 'Welcome to Milchester Medical Centre, Dr Ross.'

She blinked. It took her a few moments for the full impact of his words to become clear and finally she swallowed, about to thank him. Just then the phone rang. The brief interlude as he answered it gave her the opportunity to take a calming breath as she tried to grapple with the startling fact she was now the locum doctor at Milchester Medical Centre.

'My son,' Ben explained as he replaced the phone. 'I'm afraid he's forgotten his house keys again.' The door opened. 'Come in, Toby.' Ben gestured to Kate. 'Toby, this is Dr Ross, who'll be taking Dr Withycombe's place until Dr Neilson arrives later this year.'

Toby Buchan's thatch of black, glossy hair and silver-grey eyes were identical to his father's. Kate judged him to be about her own height, five feet seven inches, though she could see by his blazer cuffs, rapidly retreating from his wrists, that he was growing fast. 'Hello,' he said, as he held out his hand.

Kate shook it. 'Hello, Toby.'

Kate waited as Ben delved in his pocket, took out a keyring and slid one of the keys from it.

'So, the first stop, I suggest, is Lassiters,'

Ben said as he glanced back to Kate. 'It's not far, about fifteen minutes walk from here.'

'I'm walking home that way,' Toby said as he accepted the key. 'I'll show you, if you want.'

Much to her surprise, twenty minutes later Kate found herself leaving the surgery, her heart still pounding from the outcome of the interview. The paperwork and preliminaries had been organised in such a swift manner that she could hardly believe she was walking next to Toby in the soft sunshine, the last details having been finalised for her eight o'clock start on Monday morning.

In a state of mild shock, she took a deep breath. 'Are you sure you have time to show me Lassiters, Toby?' she asked a little breathlessly. 'There's no desperate rush as I'm staying with Mrs Lawrence for the time being. I could really go tomorrow.'

'Phil Lawrence's mother?' Toby's expression was equally surprised. 'I know Phil. We used to go to Milchester Junior together. He's a pupil at the comprehensive now. I'm at Milchester High, worse luck.'

'Don't you like it?' Kate asked as she followed Toby across the courtyard.

'Oh, it's OK.' Toby shrugged, but she soon became aware that the topic of school was not one of his favourites. To make conversation as they walked along, and to stop her own thoughts from whirling around her dazed

15

head, she enquired why he wasn't at school this afternoon.

'We've got a half-day because of teacher training,' he told her.

Kate laughed. 'I always wished there'd been more of those days when I was at school. Unfortunately, they seemed to be very short on the ground.'

This seemed to break the ice, and before Kate knew it she was answering a series of rapid questions, explaining she had lived and worked in London, was unmarried and had no children. This last piece of information seemed to intrigue him the most.

'What about your parents?' he asked, as they came to the busy streets of the town centre. 'Do they live in London too?'

Kate shook her head, her expression distracted for a moment. 'No, Toby, I lost my parents a long time ago. They died in a car crash when I was five.'

'Were you in the car as well?'

'No. I was staying with a neighbour at the time.'

They had come to a halt and were standing on the pavement, facing one another. Kate realised she was touched rather than offended by Ben's son's interest in her past and that, because his manner was so genuine, she didn't object to discussing something so personal. He dropped his schoolbag to the ground and frowned, obviously thinking about what she'd

16

told him, but she was surprised by his next question.

'Do you remember what your parents looked like?' For a few seconds she stood there, trying to examine, as honestly as she could, the distant and faded mental images of her mother and father.

'Well, I've a few impressions,' she admitted finally, 'rather than memories. It happened such a long time ago, Toby, that I'm not sure if they are true memories or images from photographs. My father, I know, was a very tall man and rather thin. My mother had fair hair and blue eyes.'

'Like you?' Toby's gaze moved shyly over her face and Kate smiled.

'Yes. I think so.'

He picked up his bag and threw it over his shoulder and together they resumed their journey. He asked her what had happened after the accident, his curiosity evident, and she found herself explaining that she had been fostered.

'Then, as I had no uncles or aunts,' she concluded, experiencing a familiar wave of grateful affection for her step-parents as she spoke, 'a doctor and his wife who weren't able to have children of their own decided to adopt me.'

Toby listened in silence and it wasn't until they'd come to their destination, a shop called Lassiters, that he spoke again. 'Our mother

17

died in an accident too,' he told her. 'It was on a boat. She got knocked unconscious and she didn't come round. We were only four, Tom and me, so neither of us remember what she looked like very much.' He suddenly grew embarrassed and, giving another shrug, peered into the glass window. 'I'll wait out here, if you like.'

Touched again by the way he'd apparently confided in her, Kate agreed and went into the agency. An assistant took her details, issuing her with two possible addresses, though the girl was swift to warn her that neither were what she thought Kate would require.

Twenty minutes later Kate realised she'd been right. They stood in front of one of the drab and neglected houses, paint peeling sadly from its windows and doors. 'Mega-bad,' pronounced Toby as they gazed up from the pavement.

Privately Kate didn't think they were too dreadful, compared with many properties in some parts of London, but neither could she see herself settling in such a dismal place, even for six months. The next house was in a worse state of repair and Kate felt her spirits sink to a new low. Perhaps Ben Buchan had been correct, and finding the right sort of accommodation would be impossible. However, remaining with Angie was equally impossible, given the length of time she would now be staying in Milchester.

'I'm thirsty,' Toby said suddenly as they stood in the hot sun. 'There's the cricket pitch and pavilion around the corner. We could get a drink there, if you like.'

'Sounds wonderful.' Kate sighed, pushing the depressing thoughts to the back of her mind. She followed Toby down a narrow lane and soon the sight of a pretty Edwardian pavilion and people sunbathing on the grass cheered her up. She bought two iced lemonades and they sat together on the grass in the cool shade of the trees.

Toby was talkative, telling Kate about Mrs Howard, the housekeeper who lived with them and who occupied the annexe to the house. He explained that his twin brother, Tom, and Phillip Lawrence and a boy called Peter Frost had all been good friends at junior school and the cricket pitch had once been the scene of many junior school matches.

'Tom's gone to the squash club this afternoon,' Toby added as he drank thirstily, 'otherwise he'd have used his key. And Mrs Howard is visiting her grandchildren this afternoon. We've lost three keys lately and Dad's a bit miffed so we have to pay for each new key from now on.'

Kate laughed. He was a likeable boy and she found herself enjoying his company. She parted from Toby in the high street and it took her a few minutes more to reach the surgery car park. She was just in time to see Angie

19

appear, pushing through the outer doors.

Kate grinned as they met at the Fiat. 'I start on Monday,' she told her friend, unable to disguise her excitement.

Angie hugged her. 'I told you, you had nothing to worry about with Glyn!'

Kate's eyebrows lifted ruefully. 'As a matter of fact, Glyn Withycombe wasn't here this afternoon. Dr Buchan interviewed me.'

Angie whistled through her teeth. 'What was he like?'

Kate scrambled into the Fiat, closing her door with a relieved sigh. 'Well, he gave me the job, but he made it plain he thought I might not be up to it.'

'Did he?' Angie's eyebrows lifted as she started the engine. 'You know, despite the fact he's senior partner, none of us know very much about his past. He was married once and his wife died when his twin boys were very young. And, of course, there's his affair with Mary Graham!'

Kate was about to say that she knew exactly what had happened to Ben's wife when Angie's last remark stopped her. 'Mary Graham?' she repeated slowly.

Angie nodded, raising her eyebrows and throwing Kate a rueful glance. 'Dr Mary Graham. She's a member of another practice on the other side of Milchester. They've known each other for years. Everyone says there are wedding bells ahead.'

Kate felt a strange little kick at her ribs. 'It's serious, then?'

Angie grinned and looked at her under her lashes. 'Why? Are you interested?'

Kate blushed so fiercely she felt her cheeks flaming. 'No,' she retorted too swiftly, watching Angie's eyebrows rise even further. 'Just curious, that's all.'

'Join the club!' giggled Angie and to Kate's eternal relief her friend was forced to return her concentration to her driving.

CHAPTER TWO

On Monday morning Kate drove from Angie's house at seven-thirty and arrived at Milchester Medical Centre at a quarter to eight, parking between a silver Mercedes and a Vauxhall hatchback.

The receptionist she had met on Friday was unlocking the outer doors. Lesley Shore, a woman of about her own age with neat, short brown hair, gave her a welcoming smile. 'Hi, Dr Ross. Go right ahead. Dr Buchan's in his room. Coffee's on.'

'Thanks, Lesley. Is anyone else in?' Kate walked with Lesley to the desk.

'The morning reception staff are here and Maureen Day, our practice manager, but no doctors as yet except Dr Buchan who's been on call over the weekend. Dr Greaves and Dr James, the duty doctors, will be in for their eight-thirty surgeries.'

Kate nodded. 'Have you any idea of the times of my surgeries this week?'

Lesley shook her head. 'Maureen hasn't displayed the rota yet. I'll bring a copy into you later.'

'Thanks, Lesley.' Kate made her way across the deserted reception area to the door she knew led to the corridor and then to Ben's consulting room.

When she arrived there she knocked lightly, took a breath and entered at the sound of his deep voice. He was sitting at his desk facing his computer, his fingers poised over the keyboard.

'Morning, Kate. Come in and take a seat.' Tiny creases wrinkled the corners of his eyes as he smiled and somewhat apprehensively Kate smoothed down the skirt of her smart, pale blue summer suit as she sank into the chair.

She waited as he completed his work, and when at last he turned to face her she received the full scrutiny of his dark gaze. 'Toby tells me that you had no luck with Lassiters,' he remarked.

Kate lifted her fair brows. 'Not yet, but they've given me another address.' She reached down for her bag and drew out her diary. 'A place called Hillsend. A semi-detached, two-bedroomed house on a short

22

lease.'

He frowned. 'I shouldn't trouble. They've had a lot of problems in that area recently. Half the houses are boarded up.'

'Really?' Kate was disappointed. 'You were quite right,' she acknowledged. 'Decent accommodation is proving difficult to find. I wondered if it might be worth trying further out of town.'

He looked doubtful. 'When you're on call, driving in to Milchester would be a disadvantage, especially in high summer.' He was silent for a moment, as though deep in thought, then slowly he rose to his feet and gestured to the door. 'Anyway, let's go along to Glyn's room, the one you will be occupying today since Glyn will be "floating" for the next two weeks before he leaves.'

Kate followed him into the passage and as they entered the retiring doctor's room Ben nodded to the desk. 'I think you'll find everything to hand here,' he told her, as he opened various drawers to display their contents. 'I've had a brief glance through your list and the majority of patients are those booked in from Friday and Saturday.'

'And these patients are aware they're seeing me and not Dr Withycombe?' Kate asked immediately.

'Oh, yes. They will have been informed at Reception or when the appointment was made.'

Kate gazed around her, admiring the large room with wide windows and vertical blinds, a comfortable-looking leather swivel-chair and, of course, the requisite examination couch.

'If all goes well . . .' He hesitated. 'That is . . . if you find you're settled by the end of, say, a fortnight—'

'I assure you, I have no intention of fading away,' Kate interrupted abruptly as colour rushed to her cheeks, the inference of his words being that he was still obviously doubtful of her ability to cope. Maybe she was jumping to conclusions, but she had the distinct feeling that he regarded her in a purely probationary light and that he wouldn't be surprised if she ran out of energy, rather like a damp firework, right in front of his eyes. Then she realised that she was probably falling into just such a category by sounding so defensive. Giving herself a little mental shake, she said in a more composed tone, 'I'm sure I'll find my way around, given time and a little perseverance.'

'Yes, well . . .' he began again, as he glanced at her quickly. 'If you're happy with Glyn's room then I see no reason why you shouldn't occupy it permanently. Oh, and I've arranged a general meeting of staff during the lunch-break. I think you'll find everyone pretty easy to get along with.'

Kate nodded her agreement and she watched him go. She took a deep breath as the door closed behind him, leaving a disturbing waft of aftershave in the air—a scent which she'd noticed had clung to the smart pale blue linen shirt and raven black hair. For a few seconds her heart raced and a strange mixture of apprehension and excitement flowed through her. Whatever Ben Buchan might think of her privately and despite her own deep feelings of vulnerability, she was determined to prove herself. At least he'd given her the chance—a chance she needed so badly to restore her confidence.

*   *   *

Kate studied the thermometer, then looked back at the seven-year-old boy in front of her. He was the third emergency patient inserted into her long list of patients who'd made official appointments. She'd hardly stopped to take a breath all morning, but most of her patients had been welcoming and friendly.

'Stop scratching, Sean, and let the doctor have a look at you!' Denise Markham frowned irritably at her son whose little fingers worried the rash on his arms.

Kate lifted Sean's Batman T-shirt and discovered more patches of red spots. 'How long has he had these?' she asked, glancing up at his mother.

Denise Markham shrugged. 'He woke up with a few spots four or five days ago. I assumed they were a heat rash because of the warm weather. But this morning they were even behind his ears. He'd scratched himself raw in the night. Then I thought they might be fleas from the cat.'

'So you have you a cat, Sean?' Kate asked, smiling. 'What's his name?'

'Sooty,' responded her small patient. 'But he hasn't got fleas.'

Kate nodded. 'Well, Sooty certainly isn't responsible for your spots,' she assured him and, pulling down his T-shirt, returned to her desk.

'Sean has chickenpox, Mrs Markham,' she began to explain, but was stopped short as the woman took an audible breath.

'But he's not been ill!'

Kate paused. 'I agree he seems bright enough, but he does have a temperature. I'll prescribe him some paracetamol which will reduce the fever. Cool baths and calamine lotion will help to soothe those spots.'

'Chickenpox, you say? But there's not been any at school,' the boy's mother said doubtfully.

Kate continued to process the prescription, then passed it across the desk. 'Keep Sean at home until the last crusts of the spots have dropped off, probably in about a week or maybe even ten days.'

'Ten days! But he can't be infectious for all that time!'

'The varicella-zoster virus is spread from

person to person in airborne droplets,' Kate explained. 'Children are infectious from about two days before the rash appears until about a week afterwards.'

'So Mark, my six-year-old, may have it too?'

'It's possible,' Kate agreed. 'I'd keep them both at home for this week just to be on the safe side.'

'But can't you give them antibiotics?' Mrs Markham demanded crossly.

Kate hesitated. 'There is a drug called acyclovir, which is an antiviral, but it's only used if the child is particularly unwell and, as you yourself said, Sean doesn't appear to be ill.'

Something about the woman's reaction disturbed Kate as the boy's mother knitted her eyebrows together in an angry frown. 'So you're saying you can't—or won't—give me anything to clear up Sean's spots?'

Patiently, Kate tried again. 'Chickenpox isn't something you can just "clear up", Mrs Markham. Most people have had chickenpox by the age of ten. In fact, it's more worrying in adults who've not had it. For instance, women in the final stages of pregnancy should be particularly careful.'

'So, what if I was pregnant?' Denise protested. 'Would you give the boys something then?'

'Are you pregnant?' Kate asked.

'No. But I'm very busy at work and I can't

afford to take time off.'

Kate nodded. 'Yes, I do understand—'

'How can you understand?' broke in the young woman angrily. 'It's all very well telling me to keep them off school, but it means if Mark gets it then I'll be off work for very nearly a month.'

Kate was about to enquire if there was someone who could help her with the children when the phone rang. Apologising for the interruption, she turned to answer it. Before she'd begun to answer Lesley's query Denise Markham had pulled Sean to his feet and was heading for the door.

'Please wait a moment!' Kate called, covering the mouthpiece with her hand, but in no time at all they were gone. Kate listened, distracted, as Lesley informed her that her next surgery was at four o'clock today but that Maureen had not yet completed her rota. After replacing the phone, Kate hurried into the corridor only to find it deserted. She opened the door that led into the reception area, but saw no sign of the Markhams.

Back in her consulting room she sat down, her brow furrowed. There was little more she could have done for Sean or his brother and her advice about remaining away from school would be corroborated, no doubt, by the teachers, but Denise Markham had been her first stumbling block and it unsettled her.

Managing to put the incident behind her,

she greeted her next patient, Sheila Dobson. Sheila had thin, light brown hair, was of middle age and her tired brown eyes looked out solemnly from deep sockets, but Kate was struck most by her long and rather overshot jaw. But it was her feet that Sheila Dobson was complaining about. 'They seem to have swollen,' she said bewilderedly. 'I've got blisters all over my toes.'

Kate glanced at her records and saw that Sheila had registered with the surgery eighteen months ago. Since then she'd only consulted a doctor once for a minor complaint. Kate examined her feet and, though they were large and ungainly, the toenails were trimmed and clean and the toes straight. Neither did she have dropped arches or swollen ankles. However, it was evident there *were* clusters of small blisters, both at heel and toe.

Kate discovered her patient worked as an accountant's clerk and was married with two grown-up daughters. She also noticed Mrs Dobson had trouble squeezing her feet back into her shoes.

'They look rather tight,' commented Kate, a remark to which Sheila Dobson reacted sharply.

'But I've taken size seven all my life,' protested the older woman. 'A few months ago these shoes fitted perfectly. Perhaps it's the heat.'

'Blisters are usually best left to heal on their

own and, with comfortable footwear, usually do,' Kate pointed out tactfully, 'but I'm going to book you in with our chiropodist. She may have some helpful suggestions to make.'

'If you think it will help,' said Sheila Dobson with a shrug.

'You are, other than your feet, keeping in good health, I take it?' Kate asked.

Mrs Dobson was evasive. 'Mostly, yes. Just a few headaches, but I need new glasses,' she replied. 'It's all the close work I do that plays havoc with my eyesight.'

Kate paused. 'I'd like to see you again after the chiropodist—just to make sure we haven't missed anything.' She rang through to Lesley and asked her to make Mrs Dobson's appointments. Kate was uncertain why she'd asked her patient to return, but something struck her as odd and she wanted the opportunity to speak to the woman again.

At one o'clock Tina Wyle, Lesley's fellow receptionist, called in to tell her she'd completed her list. In the staff-room Ben introduced her to Meg James. Tall and well built, Meg was a solid, handsome-looking woman in her mid-fifties who shook Kate's hand with a firm grip. As they chatted Kate knew she would get on well with her, as she would Rupert Greaves, a red-headed bachelor in his early thirties who came to join them. It was as she was talking to Meg and Rupert that Angie walked in, talking to Glyn Withycombe.

After a few moments of conversation with Glyn, Kate was disappointed to think that she only had a couple of weeks to get to know this quiet and likeable man. Together with dark-eyed, dusky-skinned Bal Chandra, they all spent a pleasurable ten minutes sampling the sandwiches which Maureen Day, the practice manager, had had delivered by outside caterers.

Then a tall, blond man entered the room and Angie squeezed Kate's arm. 'This is Damian. Remember, I told you about him.' She was whispering so that no one else could hear. 'He's quite the ladies' man. I bet you he'll be over here within seconds.'

It dawned on Kate a little later that Angie's remark was advance warning as Damian did indeed arrive to introduce himself. Promptly he engaged her in witty, ebullient conversation, as everyone else seemed to melt away except Angie. Hiding her amusement, Kate took the opportunity of seeming to listen while over his shoulder she watched Ben Buchan, a much more interesting subject, whose movements she found herself studying with increasing concentration as he talked with his colleagues.

Then, much to Kate's embarrassment, Ben suddenly met her gaze across the room. For a second or two, which felt like an eternity, she couldn't bring herself to drag her eyes away. The silvery grey gaze seemed to have locked

31

her in its grip and she swallowed. Like an adolescent, her cheeks went pink and her heart raced.

Feeling foolish, she managed to look back to Damian who seemed to be waiting for the answer to a question he must have asked. She hadn't heard a word he'd been saying, and her confusion deepened as the silence lengthened. She was saved eventually by Angie, who answered Damian's question, and thankfully, after a few minutes, the embarrassing moment was forgotten.

Later Ben joined their circle and addressed Kate directly. 'I'm about to leave on visits,' he told her as he glanced at his watch. 'I've two patients in particular who are fairly well known to each partner because of long-term problems. It's probably better if you come with me and then, should you be called out, you'll at least have some idea of their case histories.'

At that point Damian said he must leave for his calls too, and Angie headed off for the cloakrooms, leaving Kate with the distinct impression that Ben's remark about accompanying him on visits had been rather more of a command than a suggestion. With no surgery until four, she'd been looking forward to spending the afternoon in her room, leisurely reviewing her notes and generally organising herself, but as she stared into Ben's unswerving gaze it occurred to her that she could in no way refuse.

Five minutes later she found herself in the cloakroom, standing beside Angie and gazing into the mirrors above the washbasins, annoyed that she'd allowed herself to be hurried in such a way. It was after all her first day, and it seemed only sensible for her to review the morning's patients, before attempting the evening surgery. As she thought about it more she had no doubt that Ben was probably underlining the warning he'd given her at her interview—the centre was going to be a challenge for her stamina. Whatever Ben thought of her capabilities she intended to keep up with him every step of the way.

Angie, she realised, was staring at her in the mirror. 'Well, what do you think?' Angie lifted her eyebrows questioningly and for a moment Kate hesitated, unsure that she should express her reservations about Ben Buchan, even to Angie. As she was trying to decide on her answer Angie forestalled her.

'Oh, Kate, come on!' she giggled. 'What did you *really* think of our Dashing Damian?' Her eyes sparkled mischievously. 'And no fibs!'

Kate frowned into the mirror, realising her friend was on a completely different wavelength. With an inner sigh of relief Kate shrugged lightly. 'Is that what you call him?' she grinned. 'Dashing Damian?'

Angie nodded. 'Well, you must admit he's a bit of a heartthrob!'

Kate laughed. 'He looks harmless enough to me, Angie.'

'His previous two wives thought that too,' said Angie, exploding with laughter, 'before they divorced him!'

'Two?' Kate's eyes widened in mock horror. 'How old is he, for heaven's sake?'

'He's almost forty, would you believe?' related Angie, obviously enjoying her gossip. 'Two years older than Dr Buchan, in fact. But, then, Dr Buchan's had twin boys to rear and kids somehow show on your face—as you can see by this one!' They both burst into laughter again as Angie made a face in the mirror in characteristic self-mockery.

Angie chattered on as Kate applied a faint hint of eyeliner to her lower eyelids and a light touch of pink lipstick to her full, somewhat pale lips. For some reason she seemed to be more nervous of meeting Ben this afternoon than she had been at the start of the morning!

'He's a bit like Michael Douglas, don't you think?' Angie was musing as Kate slid the cosmetics back into her bag.

'Yes, I suppose so.' Kate's voice was vague. She'd barely noticed Damian's appearance, the reason being she'd been too preoccupied with someone else's!

'You're miles away.' Angie giggled again, then her face dropped. 'You're not still thinking about that wimp Julian, are you?'

'Julian? No!' In fact, Kate was secretly

34

shocked at herself as she realised that for three whole days Julian hadn't entered her head for one minute. She'd spent weeks and months actively putting him from her mind each day, and now it wasn't until Angie had mentioned him that she'd given him a thought.

'You'll find someone else,' Angie said, intending to be kind. 'Just don't let it be Damian Stewart.'

Kate laughed. 'Don't worry, men are the last thing I'm concerned with at the moment. I've enough on my hands with medicine!'

But Angie was silent now and laid her hand on Kate's arm. 'You've had a tough time, Kate. I think you're still vulnerable. Just be careful, won't you?'

Kate nodded solemnly. 'Yes, Mum.'

They both laughed, but in her heart Kate knew Angie was probably right. She was still vulnerable after Julian. He'd been everything she'd wanted in a man—she'd thought. Attentive, impressive at his job, a stimulating conversationalist. And he'd loved her—she'd thought. When they'd become engaged and had moved in together she'd imagined—no, had been *convinced*—that marriage came next on the list. How wrong she'd been!

As a lawyer, Julian had entertained on a wide scale and Kate had become accustomed to her role as hostess for the lavish dinner parties and cocktail evenings he'd given. At first she'd been impressed and flattered he'd

35

wanted her beside him. Soon, however, Julian's social life had monopolised all their free time and her own career had been regarded as a burden and hindrance.

The weekends on Julian's motor boat moored on the Thames had been what she dreaded the most. In her busy inner-city practice she'd often been on call, and inevitably there had been increasing quarrels as her own career had demanded more of her time. When she'd become ill it had seemed the final blow. No longer able to play her role in Julian's active life, their relationship had foundered.

Kate shuddered as she recalled the final day when he'd simply decided to leave their flat. Too ill with ME to be objective about the reasons for him leaving, she'd convinced herself that his suggestion to give her space had been an unselfish gesture.

It was two years now since he'd left her, and although it had taken all her will-power to recover from the double blow of illness and rejection she'd finally surfaced. And Milchester would now provide her with an opportunity to prove she was ready to continue her career, even though at this moment her heart was racing anxiously again as she thought of the coming afternoon under the critical eye of Ben Buchan.

*   *   *

36

Kate frowned as Ben took a slow right-hand turn into a long street of neglected houses.

'This is the Gower Estate—not very salubrious, I'm afraid,' he told her grimly, as they drove through a maze of tall, shabby-looking blocks of flats. 'Sanjay and Maneka Sarkar are expecting their first child. Maneka's sixteen weeks into the pregnancy after two previous miscarriages. Unfortunately, their environment isn't helping—the lift in the flats is almost always out of order and the stairs are a nightmare.'

The buildings swept by one after another in monotonous rows. Cars lined each side of the roads, some without wheels and supported by bricks, and Kate recalled with a pang of nostalgia the similarly depressing inner-city sights of graffiti-covered walls and abandoned dwellings.

'There's a chance Sanjay will soon have the offer of a flat nearer to Heathrow,' Ben continued, as they parked near a high-rise block on the northern side of the estate. 'He's a clerk at the airport and they've applied to a housing association for help.'

When the car was locked and the alarm set, they approached the ground-floor entrance, ignoring the comments of several youths who slouched against the walls, smoking and drinking. Once inside, as Ben had predicted, the lift showed no sign of operating. The dowdy concrete staircase smelt stale, but eventually, five flights up, they arrived at the Sarkars' blue painted door.

Ben knocked and within a few moments it was opened by a young man who greeted them with a wide smile. 'Dr Buchan! Please, come in.'

'This is Dr Ross, Mr Sarkar,' Ben explained as they entered. 'Dr Ross has just joined the practice as locum.'

'Welcome, Dr Ross. Please, go ahead to the bedroom.'

They followed the narrow corridor and Kate noted the exotic eastern prints on the walls, some of quite startling beauty. Maneka Sarkar lay on a double bed in a small bedroom wrapped in her robe, her feet encased in dainty embroidered slippers and her legs propped up by pillows. 'Hello, Dr Buchan,' she said, and her dark eyes went anxiously to Kate. 'Forgive me for not greeting you—I was resting.'

'I'm pleased to see it,' Ben replied, and gestured to Kate. 'This is my colleague, Dr Ross,' he said, explaining Kate's arrival once more as he sat on the edge of the bed and took out his stethoscope.

'Sit here, please, Dr Ross.' Maneka pointed to a chair and her husband drew it up for Kate.

'Mr and Mrs Sarkar have been trying for a family for five years,' Ben explained in a routine and businesslike fashion as he moved his stethoscope over Maneka's swollen abdomen. Kate was impressed at the thorough examination he made of his pregnant patient.

'I was married at seventeen, and we've always wanted children,' Maneka added, with a smile of pride at her husband who stood anxiously beside the bed. 'But we've had no luck so, as you can see, I am being very careful with this pregnancy after my two miscarriages. Have you any children, Dr Ross?'

Kate shook her head. 'I'm afraid not.'

Maneka glanced at Kate's left hand and her dark eyes opened curiously. 'Oh, I'm sorry. You're not married?'

Again Kate shook her head. 'No.'

'What happened,' Ben said swiftly, glancing at Kate, 'to worry you, Maneka?'

'I was very sick and yesterday I had cramps,' Maneka said as she looked up at Ben. 'Dr Chandra came to visit me this morning, but he said he would like you to see me too, just to make sure everything is all right.'

'Dr Chandra was quite happy with you,' Ben assured her, 'but he thinks you may have strained yourself while retching, and now I've examined you I'm inclined to agree with him.'

Maneka nodded. 'It's possible. I was so sick last week, I couldn't keep anything down.'

Ben completed his examination and, addressing Maneka in a gentle tone, he finally stood up to pack away his things. 'Hopefully the nausea will disappear, given time, but it might be an idea to try something as simple as a plain biscuit and a cup of tea before you get out of bed in the morning. It might just do the trick. You probably won't feel like it, but give it a try and see if you can keep it down.'

'Thank you, Dr Buchan.' Maneka glanced at Kate. 'It was so nice to meet you, Dr Ross. I hope I'll see you again.'

'I'm sure you will.' Kate smiled and reached out to shake the delicate hand.

Once back at the car, Ben deactivated the alarm system and they sat quietly as he scribbled a few lines on the patient notes, before returning them to the rear seat. With an abrupt turn of the head he looked at Kate, one eyebrow arched. 'What would you say are Maneka's chances of going to full term?'

Kate was taken aback by the question and for a moment she was tempted to respond that as she was not in full possession of all their patient's details her answer would be a matter of guesswork. Then, as she met his gaze, she realised that he was genuinely awaiting her reply.

'In another environment I would say very good,' she found herself answering, albeit a little hesitantly. 'She is, as far as I could gather today, healthy and looking after herself, but becoming housebound with the lift being so often out of order is a problem. But other than admitting her early, which I'm sure you've already considered, there's nothing much more to be done.'

Ben nodded slowly. 'Yes, I've tried. But Maneka is determined she wants to see the pregnancy through at home.'

Kate shrugged. 'It's strange, but I've often found the patient intuitively knows best—if there's no clinical reason to consider. Sometimes the agitation and stress from being in a hospital ward for so long a confinement can prove as much of—or even worse—a problem.'

He paused, clearly thoughtful, and then he reached out for the ignition. 'Oh, by the way, you would never be expected to make visits to the Gower Estate alone. Should you happen to have an on-call visit, you must always ring either me or one of the male staff.'

She frowned deeply. 'Is that really necessary?'

'Absolutely,' he answered sharply.

'All right, if that's the procedure.'

They drove on until the rows of dilapidated houses ended. Kate could appreciate that it might be risky to visit the estate after nightfall, but during the day the place hadn't seemed too threatening. However, she decided not to argue the point and leaned back in her seat.

After a while Kate noticed they'd joined the motorway. Several junctions later a gentle gradient took them over a bridge and past the garden of a cottage surrounded by fruit trees.

'Splinters Cottage is the home of Hugh

Conway and his wife, Sara,' Ben explained, as they left the slip road and approached the drive, which was overlooked by the motorway. 'Hugh is ex-army and suffers from post-traumatic stress disorder, though we have never been able to identify the precise cause of his sickness. He was an officer involved in special duties during his career. The army retired him when he began to show signs of severe stress.'

'So he's without a job?' Kate asked.

'Yes, spends his time growing roses now, lucky man.' Ben grinned, and Kate was struck by the difference his smile made to the contours of his face. His silvery eyes sparkled and the glint of white even teeth made her take a breath. 'Sara's the breadwinner,' he continued, and Kate was grateful for the few seconds more in which, surreptitiously, she was able to examine the profile of the cleanshaven features and strong, square chin.

'Sara commutes to the City to her job in advertising,' he went on, unaware of her gaze. 'Over the last few months Hugh has shown signs of recovery after his treatment with a local psychiatrist, David Bright. However, Sara rang in this morning and asked for a visit. I've no idea what it's about.'

Kate noted he referred to the couple by their first names and wondered if they were personal friends as well as patients, but she had no time to discover any more as the door was opened swiftly after their first knock. An attractive-looking woman in her mid-thirties with cropped fair hair, dressed in a sweatshirt and jeans, beckoned them in.

Dipping their heads under the low beams of the cottage, they followed Sara Conway to a small, book lined study where her husband sat in an armchair. The curtains were half-drawn against the sunlight but even in the gloom Kate could see that Hugh Conway looked ill.

Dressed in a grubby open-necked shirt and with a heavy growth of beard around his jaw, he passed a shaking hand across his damp forehead. 'Sorry to have brought you out here, Ben,' he apologised, not appearing to notice Kate. 'Can't drive at present with this.'

Ben sat beside him, and as he began to speak to Hugh Kate felt someone touch her arm. She turned and Sara suggested they adjourned to another room. Kate followed her into the kitchen and finally through to the back garden where she took a breath at the multitude of roses that grew there.

'They're beautiful!' Kate breathed in the overpowering scent of the blooms. 'So fragrant!'

Sara nodded. 'Hugh grows them—it's his passion and therapy. He seems to have green fingers as well as a natural love of flowers.' She walked on and Kate accompanied her, bending to smell the roses as she moved slowly along the path.

'I wonder if you'll give these to Ben for me?' Sara said abruptly, stopping to pass Kate a small brown bottle. 'I'm afraid I found them in Hugh's drawer this morning. They're sleeping pills, I think—at least they look like the ones my husband usually takes. He already has a supply in the bathroom and, before discovering these, I thought them to be the only sleeping pills in the house. Hugh has taken quite a variety of drugs over the last few years. I could be wrong, but I usually keep a strict check on what we have in the house.'

Kate turned the bottle over. 'There's no label on them. Are they prescribed by Dr Buchan?' She unscrewed the cap and tipped the drugs into her palm.

'He has medication for his insomnia, yes, but from his consultant psychiatrist. The problem is that several weeks ago he had a violent nightmare, more violent than the usual ones. There was no way I could reassure him afterwards and we haven't slept properly since because of the reaction. He's in a perpetual sweat and he can't stop shaking. It goes without saying that he's deeply depressed and ... er ...' She fumbled for the right words. 'He doesn't seem quite in a rational state of mind.' She sighed, looking up slowly. 'I haven't been into work, of course.'

Kate examined the pills and decided Sara was probably right about them being a medication for insomnia. 'Have you

44

mentioned to your husband that you've found these?' she asked.

Sara shook her head and the lines of stress etched across her attractive face deepened. 'No. You see, I'm worried he might try to do something silly when he has one of these attacks. I can't face another row if he flatly denies knowing about them.'

Kate knew very little of the Conways, but it was evident that Sara was coping with a particularly difficult situation, possibly even dangerous, if Hugh's balance of mind was disturbed. Kate replaced the pills in the bottle and slid them into her pocket, telling Sara that she'd talk to Ben on her behalf at the first opportunity.

Back in the cottage, Ben met them in the kitchen. 'I've given Hugh a relaxant,' he told Sara, 'and he'll probably sleep now. But I'm going to ring David Bright and ask him to visit you as soon as possible.'

Sara nodded, her face drawn and weary as she made an effort to smile. 'Thank you, Ben. Actually, I've just been talking to Dr Ross—' A noise from the study made them turn and Sara glanced nervously at Kate.

Hugh suddenly appeared, his gait unsteady. Ben moved towards him, suggesting he went upstairs to rest, but Hugh was reluctant to comply and said he'd wait to see them off.

Back in the Mercedes, Kate looked at the cottage and felt a strong pang of sympathy for

Sara, a thought which seemed to be echoed by Ben as he slid across his seat belt and buckled it. 'Hugh was very disorientated today,' he remarked worriedly. 'I'm afraid this indicates a relapse after such a promising start to the year.'

It was not until they were out of sight of the cottage and back onto the motorway that Kate drew the bottle from her pocket and explained what Sara had told her. Ben glanced down quickly and she could see by his expression that this new development indicated even more of a dilemma than he'd anticipated.

They travelled in silence for a while and Kate knew that Ben was deep in thought so she made no attempt to converse. As the signs for Milchester advised the motorist to leave the motorway at the next junction, Kate glanced at her watch. 'I've half an hour before surgery and there may be something new in at Lassiters,' she murmured distractedly, her thoughts also still with the Conways. 'Perhaps I'll call in there on our way through town. Could you drop me off, do you think, and I'll walk back to the centre?'

She was quite unprepared for his answer as slowly he shook his head, apparently bringing himself back from the problem of the Conways. 'Before you do that,' he said, his grey eyes regaining their usual silvery glimmer of attention, 'I've had an idea which may be of interest to you. I haven't time to go into it now,

46

but I'll catch you at six after surgery—if that's convenient?'

She could hardly say no, she realised, but what could he possibly have to say that bore any relevance to a visit to Lassiters? Nevertheless, she agreed and they flashed swiftly past the town centre signs, with the tantalising prospect of the remainder of the afternoon stretching ahead of her before her curiosity could be satisfied.

CHAPTER THREE

Kate completed her surgery a few minutes before six, gathered the notes on her desk and took them to Reception where Jocylyn March and Hilly Lang, the two young afternoon receptionists, were deep in conversation.

'Dr Buchan has taken three extra patients this evening,' Hilly was explaining to Jocylyn as they checked the computer screen, 'so, with two more to go, I would think he'll be roughly another quarter of an hour.'

Kate stepped forward, her brow creasing at what she'd overheard. 'What is the procedure for seeing extra patients, Hilly?' she asked.

The young receptionist hesitated. 'Well, if there are any, normally the doctors take it in turns. It works out at about one week in every six for each member of staff.'

47

'And when is my turn?' Kate asked.

Hilly paused again. 'Actually, your name isn't included as yet, Dr Ross.'

Kate looked at Hilly in surprise. 'But why?'

Hilly shook her head. 'I'm not sure. Perhaps it's because Dr Withycombe is still with us.'

Kate leaned forward, narrowing her eyes at the computer screen as Hilly scrolled downwards. 'You have Dr Buchan's name down here twice—this week and next. I think you should insert mine as from next Monday. It seems only fair.'

Hilly looked doubtful. 'I'm not sure Dr Buchan would like me to make such a change without consulting him.'

'Don't worry, I'll take responsibility,' Kate assured her.

Still seeming a little reluctant, Hilly began to input Kate's name and Kate left to return to her room. She didn't understand why she'd been omitted, and at the earliest opportunity she would bring up the matter with Maureen, who organised the rotas.

Giving it no more thought, she brushed out her blonde hair to a silky bob. She applied a coat of fresh, pale peach lipstick, using her small hand mirror. When she walked into Reception again the desk had closed and the waiting room was deserted.

Kate decided to wait outside in the warm evening sunshine. She sat on the wooden bench in the garden as the glorious evening

48

warmth engulfed her. Scents of the flowers permeated the air and she breathed it in slowly, her thoughts once again returning to Ben and the reason he wanted to talk to her.

'Sorry to keep you,' a deep voice said, suddenly rousing her out of her thoughts. 'How was your afternoon?'

Ben's sudden approach through the garden caused her to feel oddly stirred, but she smiled and moved along the bench in order to give him room to sit beside her. 'It went without too many hitches, I think,' she was pleased to be able to tell him, and briefly she outlined some of her patients, though as she was so curious as to what he was about to say she decided not to go into detail.

He nodded thoughtfully and then smiled at her. 'I expect you're wondering what all this is about?'

'Yes, I am rather intrigued,' she agreed.

'To be frank, Kate, I don't hold out much hope of Lassiters providing you with anything particularly interesting, and I wouldn't like to see you have to settle for anything less,' he told her.

Kate had arrived at the same conclusion herself, although she'd resigned herself to the fact she might have to take something like the first house she'd seen with Toby should nothing else prove to be available. However, she said nothing and waited for him to continue.

'I also feel that if you were forced to look further out of town it would be inconvenient for work and certainly time-consuming,' he went on, pausing as he looked at her. 'So, with this in mind, I'm about to make a suggestion which is intended to benefit both you and the practice, but—I stress—there's absolutely no obligation . . .'

By this time Kate was so intrigued she was holding her breath. She simply couldn't imagine what was coming next.

'So . . .' he hesitated again ' . . . there is one alternative. The Den.'

She looked at him blankly. 'The Den?'

He nodded. 'It's only two small rooms plus a kitchen and a bathroom, and it doesn't comprise a palace, but—'

'I'm sorry,' she interrupted him, laughing softly, 'you've lost me. The Den? Where is this?'

He paused, raising his brows as though he thought she might already have known. 'Oh, didn't I say? The Den is a flat over a workshop in the grounds of my house. I'm sorry, I should have explained.'

Kate hesitated, unsure if she'd understood correctly. 'A flat? But surely you must use it for some purpose?'

'Yes, in a sense,' he agreed. 'The boys have a lot of their junk stored there. And I do use the workshop below, but only infrequently these days.' He shrugged. 'As I've said, if you're not interested—'

'Oh, yes, I am.' Kate was just trying to recover from the shock. 'It sounds wonderful. I'd really begun to think I'd have to settle for one of those houses near the town centre.'

'Well, it's nothing special but it is warm and cosy and quite modern.' He frowned. 'Anyway, have a look at it first. Come at the weekend, if you like. Saturday, shall we say? I'm off duty then.'

They agreed on one o'clock and Kate couldn't help but wonder just how long and hard he'd thought over the offer before he'd decided to make it.

He lifted his case and rose, then frowned, turning back to her. 'Oh, by the way, I phoned David Bright and he's calling on the Conways first thing tomorrow. Perhaps he'll be able to shed some light on what has happened to Hugh.' He smiled—rather uncertainly, she thought. 'Well, goodnight, Kate.'

'Goodnight, Ben.'

After he'd gone Kate remained a few minutes more to think over what had just happened. She found it quite hard to believe she'd been so lucky. Eventually she took the path that led to the car park, and as she unlocked her car she turned in time to see the Mercedes drive past.

Inside her car she sat quite still, unable to believe that Ben Buchan had just provided the answer to a very big problem but, then, she

51

reflected ruefully, a female locum doctor, post-ME and minus accommodation, was probably more of a potential headache than even he'd bargained for!

*   *   *

'It's through the old town and you take the first left off to Deer Lane,' explained Angie on Saturday morning, scrutinising Kate's pretty pale blue summer dress and the way it fell gently over her slender hips. 'But you'll have to be careful—the lanes there go off in all directions and it's easily missed.'

'Don't worry.' Kate smiled. 'Dr Buchan sketched the directions for me.'

Angie lifted her brows. 'Did he, indeed?'

Kate blushed and made a bolt for the front door, knowing she'd aroused her friend's curiosity. True to form, Angie was right behind her as she hesitated on the door-step. 'You know,' she said frowningly, 'Dr Buchan's such a private man. He's the last person I'd have expected to make such an offer.'

Kate tried to make light of this. 'Well, I think he must have taken pity on me,' she joked, but she could see Angie wasn't convinced.

As she drove to Deer Lane she admitted to herself that she was as surprised as Angie. All she could think was that the arrangement would benefit him if the efficiency of the

52

practice was all-important, as she suspected it was.

Casting her mind back over the week, she felt that in general her surgeries had been successful. Denise Markham had been the single cause of her concern and although she'd half-expected another visit—indeed, would have preferred to see her again—she'd heard nothing more. So, other than the Markhams, the transition of Glyn's patients had been smooth enough . . .

However, her feeling of optimism was soon tested as she approached Ben's house. Doubts had begun to set in over his offer of accommodation. For instance, would he find himself reluctant to use his workshop if she should accept the offer of The Den? Would the arrangement, once known, become the source of gossip?

Kate was so lost in thought she missed the junction of the road Angie had warned her about and, annoyed with herself, she pulled in to a lay-by a little further along. She glanced at the map Ben had drawn her and realised she'd taken the wrong turning. Finding her way back, she finally came to the confusing intersection of main roads and lanes. Turning right into the one Ben had indicated, she was relieved to see, half-obscured by foliage, the name Deer Lane.

Number thirty-nine was halfway along and, giving a small sigh of relief, Kate drove into the narrow sandy drive bordered by trees. She was just admiring the peaceful setting when suddenly two figures jumped out from the bushes in front of her, waving and shouting.

'Dr Ross! This way!' called one of the boys, presumably Toby, who was wearing a blue T-shirt. The other boy had on a red one. Kate wound down the window of her Volkswagen, intending to speak to them, but they both charged off, laughing. Smiling to herself, Kate drove after them.

The Buchans' home, appearing suddenly at the end of the drive, was a rambling, but endearingly solid-looking Victorian property. A huge black dog lay panting by the front door.

'He's perfectly harmless,' a voice called as Kate pulled up, and she smiled as Ben's tall figure approached. He was dressed casually in jeans and checked shirt, his broad shoulders swaying in a relaxed manner she hadn't seen before. 'The most Caesar will do is get under your feet. You found us, then?' He grinned as he bent to peer in the window. 'We were beginning to wonder if you'd got lost. The boys were just setting off to find you.' He reached down and opened her door for her. 'It wouldn't be the first time we've had to reclaim our visitors from another road.'

She laughed. 'Oh, well, better late than never. What a lovely house!'

'We don't think so in autumn when we're

buried under leaves,' he said with a chuckle, and Kate looked up to see a flash of strong, white teeth under a broad smile, once again transforming his features into a startlingly handsome face.

She clambered out and stared up at the old building, its walls bearing heavy curtains of the kind of thick green ivy that would turn red in autumn. 'I should think it's worth it,' she said quietly, and he nodded.

'Come along and we'll have a look at The Den first,' he suggested, and she followed his lead along the little pebble path that led under the low branches of a line of beech trees.

'The previous owner had this flat-cum-garage built to accommodate his gardener-chauffeur,' Ben explained in a tone of wry amusement as they approached a house in miniature with a pointed roof and two square windows set above an up-and-over garage door. 'He was rather an eccentric, I gather. Had a classic Bentley which was the love of his life. The entrance to the flat is at the rear. Just watch your step as you round the corner—I've got to even up the path.'

Carefully skirting the outer wall, she came face to face with the twins. Kate still couldn't tell the difference between Toby and his brother, save for the colour of their T-shirts. Ben immediately made introductions, but in the next instant the boys had leapt up the stairs after Ben had unlocked the back door.

At the top of the stairs, Kate found herself gazing into a small, bright living room with a window that gave out onto a canopy of trees.

Ben lifted his eyebrows. 'Sofa, dresser, telephone extension,' he rattled off as they passed through and into the kitchen. 'Small . . .' he shrugged ' . . . but well equipped.'

'Mrs Howard's had an electric blanket on it to air it,' Tom said, as once in the bedroom, he forgot himself and bounced on the bed, before receiving a frown from his father.

'We cleared out all our stuff,' Toby announced, and opened the door of the cupboards, one by one, to prove it.

'The shower doesn't work!' Tom was pleased to reveal as they all peered into the bathroom. 'And the bathplug's missing.'

'A couple of jobs I've yet to do,' Ben growled, giving his son another frown. 'But thank you for the reminder.'

Kate laughed as he bundled them from the room and they went leaping back down the stairs.

'While you reflect on what you might be letting yourself in for by coming to stay here, with two exuberant adolescents crashing around the place . . .' Ben grinned as they stood on the landing ' . . . let's have some lunch on the terrace.'

This was totally unexpected and ten minutes later she found herself seated at a large, white, wrought-iron garden table, being served crisp

56

jacket potatoes by Tom and lemonade by Toby. She hadn't imagined the day would turn out half so pleasurably. The meal was punctuated by jokes and peals of laughter and a rather strange, tummy-turning sensation whenever she glanced at Ben and found him smiling at her.

After the meal she helped to carry the dishes to the kitchen. The dishwasher was left to do its job and they resumed their seats on the terrace. The boys decided to occupy themselves on the grass tennis court and Kate gazed admiringly around the garden. 'Have you always lived here?' she couldn't resist asking.

A fleeting shadow went over his face as he paused. 'Since the boys were six. My wife and I lived in Surrey for two years when we came back from South Africa where we'd been working as doctors for a charity organisation. After Paula died I decided we needed a fresh start. I looked around for somewhere I thought would be a good place for the boys to grow up and for a suitable practice. Milchester seemed to fit the bill.'

'Toby and Tom were born in South Africa?'

'Yes, and it's a beautiful country. But I wanted something more secure for them. I suppose I missed England enough to decide that our future lay here.'

Kate wondered what his wife had been like and thought how tremendously difficult it must have been for him to continue alone.

Almost as if answering her thoughts, he went on, 'My parents, who are retired and live in Christchurch, came to Surrey and spent a lot of time with Toby and Tom after the accident. The boys stay in Christchurch each summer for a few weeks—Dad takes them fishing and my mother spoils them hopelessly.' He shrugged. 'A little spoiling every now and then does them no harm. Lord only knows, they deserve it.'

It must have been a terrible ordeal to lose a wife at such a young age, Kate thought sadly, for not only did he have his own grief to contend with but the boys' too. 'Toby explained his mother had been involved in a boating accident,' she said quietly.

For a moment he looked surprised that she knew and then he nodded. 'The boom fractured her skull. By the time they got her to hospital there was no hope of recovery.' Then, pulling back his shoulders, he shrugged again. 'Anyway, enough about us. What about you?'

Kate admired his lack of self-pity, but he hadn't prevented her from seeing the flicker of sadness in his eyes as he'd talked of his wife. Perhaps it was this that made her tell him about her engagement to Julian, something she wouldn't have spoken of normally— certainly not to someone she'd known for such a short time—but as she talked his soft grey eyes rested on her with quiet attentiveness.

It was still difficult, she realised, to be objective about Julian. The ME had brought her so low, physically and mentally, she hadn't had time to deal with the feelings of betrayal over their failed engagement. Even now, she realised, they still surfaced and it was that which had caused her to feel so vulnerable.

The boys' voices rang in the still air as the sun was slowly obscured from view by low, hazy cloud, and suddenly she shivered. She felt a mixture of panic and alarm as she realised she'd been talking at length and Ben was sitting opposite her, his eyes not having left her face.

'I'm sorry,' she apologised flusteredly, looking at her watch. 'I didn't realise it was getting so late. I've taken up all of your Saturday afternoon.'

He grinned. 'You've actually saved me a rather energetic couple of hours. I had the perfect excuse not to agree to an afternoon of rather fraught tennis.'

She smiled as she rose to her feet. 'Well, in that case, all I can do is thank you again for the offer of The Den—and accept!'

'Good.' He stood facing her, his silvery eyes sparkling in the reflection of the late sunshine.

Kate still felt in a daze as she gazed at him. He was offering her the perfect answer to her problem so why, then, was she feeling so . . . disturbed? Was it perhaps because she was so attracted to the idea that the strength of the appeal unnerved her? Kate gave herself another mental shake and told herself it was the sensible thing to do. There was no reason why the arrangement couldn't work out very well. All she had to do was to make sure she didn't intrude into his private life—as she was sure he wouldn't intrude into hers.

It was a thought she was forced to ponder as, after having said her goodbyes to the twins and Ben, just as she was driving away a large vehicle passed her in the drive and pulled up on the other side of the Mercedes. In her mirror Kate saw a young woman climb out of a Land Rover.

Kate was struck by her attractive, dark-haired appearance and her immaculate short tennis dress with a sweater slung casually around her shoulders as she lifted her face to Ben's.

*   *   *

Kate related her good news to the Lawrences that night and they celebrated with Angie's speciality, paella. After the family had gone to bed Kate and Angie shared a nightcap in the kitchen. Kate mentioned casually the visitor she'd seen at Ben's house.

'Oh, that sounds like Mary Graham,' said Angie. 'Quite a stunner, isn't she?'

Kate merely nodded. She didn't want Angie to see she was unduly interested, and she wasn't—was she? However, as Kate washed her mug and put it away in the cupboard Angie insisted on revealing what she knew of Mary Graham who was, it transpired, a regular visitor to the surgery.

Kate eventually changed the subject, despite the curiosity she had to admit she undoubtedly felt regarding the female doctor. It was a curiosity that continued right up to the point of sleep. Even after completing a tense chapter of a novel she had been longing to read, her thoughts stubbornly strayed back to Mary Graham.

*　　　*　　　*

Sunday dawned, and in a flurry of hugs and kisses Angie and the children waved her goodbye. As Ben was out on call when Kate arrived, Mrs Howard, who had arrived back from visiting her grandchildren, took her into the house and made a pot of tea, setting out the china on the large kitchen table and telling Kate to sit down and catch her breath before she started her unpacking.

'Dr Buchan employed me when my husband died,' she told Kate as she sliced a sponge cake. 'The boys needed someone to look after them when he was out on call and I was at a loose end. To be honest, it was a life-saver, coming here. Although,' she added, as she set the sponge on plates, 'my daughter has a little girl of four and she's always on at me to go and live with her in Oxford. The point is, I do like my independence.'

The twins came bursting into the kitchen, but with one glance at Mrs Howard's raised eyebrows they sat quietly at the table. To Kate's great amusement they tucked into the cake without a word, and Mrs Howard gave Kate a wink.

'We'll help with your cases,' Toby said as soon as he'd finished.

'Hinder more like,' commented Mrs Howard with a rueful grin.

Toby and Tom carried her cases up to The Den and Kate's moving-in went without a hitch—so much so that in no time at all they were all back in the kitchen for another round of tea and a second helping of sponge.

'Come for supper,' Toby said, as Kate finally got up to leave.

'Yes,' agreed Mrs Howard, 'as it's your first evening, I'm sure Dr Buchan would have asked you himself.'

But Kate politely refused, saying she still had plenty of unpacking to do. She intended to start as she meant to go on and not encroach on the Buchans' hospitality. To her own confusion, she found she had vague mental pictures of Mary Graham arriving and awkward responses all around. So, much to the twins' disappointment, she returned to The Den and began to make herself comfortable in her new home.

It was late on Sunday evening when she had just begun to soak in a bath—now fitted with a plug—that she suddenly remembered the changes she'd instructed Hilly to make on the computer. With all that had happened, it had completely escaped her mind. Tempted to ring Ben—who might still have a certain lady visitor with him—she decided against it. To be pestered at home by a phone call on her very first night would hardly be an auspicious beginning to her tenancy!

*   *   *

As Kate drew the blind in the small living room the sun spilled into the room like molten gold. She blinked the sleep from her eyes. It took a few moments to adjust herself to her new surroundings then, humming contentedly, she went to the kitchen in search of breakfast.

Kate felt better than she had done for months. She dressed in a slim-fitting navy blue skirt and a pretty peach blouse, pulling her freshly washed blonde hair back from her face into a golden knot. Her pale complexion was slowly tanning to a golden beige and her blue eyes sparkled.

Satisfied with her appearance, she gathered her bag and case and made her way to the Volkswagen parked in the drive. There was another double garage to the right of the house and Ben had given her a key should she wish to garage her car.

This morning, as she'd expected, the Mercedes was gone. Caesar barked inside the house and Mrs Howard, who was shaking a duster from an upstairs window, waved. The boys, Kate reflected, must have left for school as there was no sudden burst of activity from the front door.

When Kate arrived at work at eight-thirty, Ben had already started his surgery. Deciding she would catch Maureen at lunchtime to explain about the computer changes, she took coffee into her room and attended to her post. Then, switching on her machine, she brought up her first patient's name, surprised to discover it was Sara Conway.

When Sara walked in, Kate thought she looked terrible, with dark rings beneath her eyes and a sallow, tired-looking complexion. Sara didn't comment on her husband. She'd come, she explained, about herself.

'I've been having excessively heavy periods,' she said with a sigh, 'with more and more discomfort. It's a kind of bearing-down sensation that radiates back into my spine.'

Kate examined Sara and decided that she was probably suffering from a condition known as endometriosis.

'What in heaven's name is that?' Sara asked as she pulled on her sweater.

'The theory goes that fragments of the

lining of the uterus locate themselves in other parts of the body, usually in the pelvic cavity,' Kate explained as she resumed her seat at the desk. 'The exact cause of endometriosis is unknown but it's thought that some part of the menstrual flow doesn't manage its natural passage away from the body. Instead, it travels to the Fallopian tubes and into the pelvic cavity.'

'Which is why I've had the pain?' Sara asked as she sat down.

Kate nodded. 'Yes, it can be most unpleasant and you may be recommended to have a laparoscopy—an examination of the abdominal cavity. This examination is done under general anaesthetic and the laparoscope—an illuminated viewing tube— provides us with direct visualisation of the tubes and ovaries.'

Sara frowned. 'And after the laparoscopy— if endometriosis is diagnosed?'

'Well, your consultant may advise progestogen drugs or even a combined oral contraceptive to prevent menstruation. On the other hand, a woman who doesn't want a family or who's nearing menopause might consider a hysterectomy.'

Sara nodded, deep in thought. Then she said quietly, 'I don't want to worry Hugh with this, Dr Ross, for obvious reasons. I think it would be too much for him to cope with at the moment.'

65

Kate nodded slowly. 'How is your husband?'

'David Bright saw him last week.' Sara gave an uncertain shrug. 'He's changed his medication and I thought Hugh seemed a little better . . . but my confidence has been rocked since finding those tablets. David Bright mentioned them to Hugh and his response was to say they were out-of-date sleeping pills from years ago. I suppose he could be telling the truth.'

Kate paused, reluctant to comment. 'I'll do what I can to hurry the appointment along for you,' she said with concern, 'and you should receive it shortly—it will come direct to you.'

'Thank you, I'll look out for it.' Sara stood up. 'To be honest, it's wonderful to have a female doctor. I would have come before but I know Dr James is rushed off her feet and Ben has his work cut out with Hugh.'

Kate smiled. 'If you're worried at any point, please come in and see me.'

After she left, Kate reflected on Sara's plight. The marriage was under a great deal of stress and she wondered, not for the first time, what the relationship between Ben and the Conways was.

At midday she saw a youngster of thirteen, Peter Frost, and Kate wondered if this was the friend that Toby had talked of. He was accompanied by his aunt, Betty Mowbray, a woman in her early forties. Kate learned from Mrs Mowbray that Peter's parents had divorced a year previously.

'Peter's mother—my sister—and my niece have gone to live in Oxford,' she explained as she sat beside her nephew. 'Peter's older brother is living with his father in London and Peter's living with us for a while, but he's had to have a lot of time off school lately—he's at Milchester High. He's always so tired!'

Kate looked at the boy, and when she asked him how he felt he shrugged, his shoulders drooping, a gesture that prompted his aunt to raise her eyebrows and sigh as if to emphasise the point she'd made.

'I'm sort of achy,' Peter finally said, indicating his legs. 'I get a lot of headaches, too, and I feel sick,' he added. 'It's just all over everywhere that I don't feel right.'

'He could go to sleep at any time,' his aunt agreed. 'We've seen the school nurse, but it's done no good. They just say he'll have to try harder at things like sports and games.'

Kate studied Peter's records, discovering nothing to indicate what might be wrong although, during his parents' divorce, he'd been referred to a child psychologist.

'Peter, go and wait for me in the waiting room as the doctor's finished with you,' his aunt said. When he'd gone she leaned across the desk, lowering her voice in a confidential manner. 'My husband and I think it's all because of the divorce. Peter has come off the worst of all the kids. He's more sensitive and has taken the split to heart. Besides which, though my husband and I are happy to have him, he should be with his rightful parents. If you ask me, all this tiredness and sickness is in his mind.'

'You mean, a psychosomatic illness?' Kate suggested.

Mrs Mowbray nodded. 'Well, it could be. It's been going on for a long time now.'

'Is there any hope of Peter being reunited with either of his parents?' Kate murmured thoughtfully.

'Not in the near future. My sister is living with my mother and Peter's father is living with the older boy in London somewhere.'

Kate glanced again at the records, frowning. 'I see Peter had a severe bout of flu when he was about eleven.'

Mrs Mowbray nodded. 'Just after he started senior school. It was after that things got really bad. A kid who can't play football and bursts into tears at the least little thing isn't healthy, to my mind. At junior school Peter and my Eric were football-crazy, the pair of them.'

Kate nodded slowly. 'And the problems seem to stem from this time?'

'Yes, I would say so, though I hadn't thought of it like that, I must say.'

Kate came to a decision. 'Mrs Mowbray, I'd like to examine Peter thoroughly and go over his history in detail. Could you bring him in tomorrow if I make a longer appointment?'

Mrs Mowbray frowned. 'It would have to be after three when I finish work.'

'That will be fine. See you tomorrow, then.' Kate led the way to Reception and arranged for a late-afternoon appointment. When she returned to her room she found Ben waiting for her just inside the door.

'I'd like to speak to you,' he said rather abruptly.

She glanced at her list. 'I've no one waiting at the moment—' She broke off as a woman in a red blouse appeared at the door. Kate nodded. 'Oh, hello, Mrs Pearce.'

Ben acknowledged the woman and, saying he'd catch Kate later, left the room.

'Mrs Pearce for her BP and medication check,' said Jocylyn. The small lady hurried across and sat in the patient's chair and began her litany of aches and pains, giving Kate no time to reflect on what possibly could have so upset Ben.

At one o'clock, eager to resolve the problem, she checked his consulting room, but Jocylyn explained he'd left for a lunchtime house call. So it wasn't until a quarter to three that Kate finally caught up with him in his room.

He was sitting in his chair, and when she knocked he glanced up. 'Come in,' he said sharply, and Kate knew she hadn't been mistaken earlier. There *was* something wrong.

As she took a seat, he slid a piece of paper

across the desk. Kate recognised it as a computer printout. Her eyes swept over it and she saw it was the details of the extra patients slotted onto the end of surgery, with her name at the top of the list.

'I can explain—' she began, and then stopped as she saw he was in no mood for explanations—explanations which she should have given last week when she'd authorised Hilly to go ahead and make the changes but which she'd forgotten about until the previous night.

'I'm afraid it's too late for explanations,' Ben said sharply. 'It was Hilly who took the measure of my annoyance this morning when I discovered the rotas had been changed.'

Kate sighed. 'I'd been meaning to speak to Maureen,' she said, angry at herself for her incompetence. 'I thought it might have been a mistake—'

'We check the schedules very carefully before they go out,' Ben said, his frown deepening. 'There was no mistake, Kate.'

'But your name was inserted twice,' Kate persisted, still unable to grasp his meaning.

'As I intended,' he answered abruptly, and she stared at him, still confused. 'For the time being, I'd decided not to include you on the evening extras—a decision which I'd discussed fully with Maureen.'

'But why?' Kate frowned, keenly aware she must be missing the point.

70

'Well, in my judgement, I felt for the next six weeks we could see how things panned out. You've recently recovered from a debilitating illness and the extra patients who are added to the end of the day's list can be time-consuming and exhausting. I was quite prepared to cover this week and I'm sure the other members of staff—'

'But I couldn't possibly accept that!' Kate interrupted, horrified to think that other members of staff would be expected to perform her duties. 'I assured you I was fit enough for the job. I understood from the start that the pressures would be exacting. If, as Hilly explained, we all take our fair share of those extras who can't be seen during the day, then I expect to be included on that rota.'

'It's for me to do what *I* think is best, Kate.' His tone was firm. 'No matter what you thought at the time, it was not up to you to alter the database on the computer. The reception staff know their jobs and do them efficiently. If you had a problem with something, you should have spoken to me—or Maureen—first.' He leaned back in his chair, turning a pen in his long brown fingers.

'And there's something else . . . One of your patients, a Mrs Denise Markham, has made a complaint through Rupert Greaves who made a house call to see her younger son late on Friday evening. He administered an antiviral to the younger boy, Mark, who was ill with

71

chickenpox. Afterwards Mrs Markham expressed her concern that Sean, whom you'd seen during the week, had also been sick and had warranted an antiviral which you'd refused to give.'

'Did Dr Greaves see Sean that evening?' Kate asked.

'No, just the younger boy.'

'And Sean has seen no other doctor since his mother brought him in to see me?'

'As far as the records reveal—no.'

'Which can only mean Sean has recovered —as I expected he would. In my judgement, Sean had a slightly raised temperature but was otherwise well, and certainly not ill enough to give an antiviral to. As I explained to Mrs Markham, there was a possibility Mark might catch it and it would be wise to keep both boys at home. I'm afraid she wasn't satisfied with this suggestion and left while I was speaking on the telephone to Lesley.'

Ben considered this, his head bent. 'I'll see her myself when she comes in,' he murmured after a while. 'I'm afraid Rupert received another version of what happened.' He sighed and laid down the pen. 'And, as you say, Sean appears to have made the recovery you anticipated . . .'

Kate was silent for a moment, then realised that even if the question of Denise Markham's complaint had been resolved, the matter of the late extras had not.

'I apologise,' Kate said quietly, 'for asking Hilly to change the information on the computer, and I regret not having consulted you first. I'll see Hilly afterwards and make an apology personally. However, I must insist that the correction stands and that I take my share of late extras. I'm employed as locum for Glyn Withycombe and there's no reason, medical or otherwise, why I should not fulfil all my duties.'

She had no idea what he was thinking as he continued to regard her, his face revealing no clue, his grey eyes impassive. 'Very well,' he said eventually. 'Though I trust that if anything else meets with your dissatisfaction you'll approach me first to discuss it before hastening to change it.'

Fully aware of the irony in the warning, Kate nodded and rose from her seat. 'Of course,' she replied. As she was about to leave she decided that there was one problem which, in view of their conversation, she would be wise to mention.

'There is something . . .' she began, her gaze meeting his. 'I saw a young boy of thirteen today—Peter Frost. He's a pupil at Milchester High, apparently, and, I think, a friend of Toby's.'

Ben's face was suddenly alert. 'Yes, that's right, he is.'

'According to his aunt, Peter has exhibited symptoms of abnormal fatigue, poor concentration and nausea. She says he's often very close to tears and could sleep at any time. I managed to trace some of these symptoms back to when Peter was eleven and had flu, just after he started at Milchester High.'

'Has he had any routine blood tests lately?' Ben asked with a frown.

Kate shook her head. 'None since the flu. But I'm anxious to take some tomorrow when he comes in for a longer appointment.'

'Any ideas?'

Kate nodded. 'Yes, I think Peter may be a candidate for ME.' She waited uncertainly, but since he continued to stare at her, saying nothing, she went on. 'Many doctors recognise ME as a potentially severely debilitating illness with an organic basis—other doctors are less convinced. My point is, should Peter need long-term treatment for ME I'd like to be able to refer him to someone else within the practice when I leave—someone with whom I've been conferring and who'll be sympathetic to the case.'

'When is Peter coming in again?'

'At a quarter past four tomorrow,' Kate answered directly. 'Your surgery ends at four, which would just give you time—'

'To see your young patient?' he suggested, and Kate nodded.

'All right, I'll try to be there,' he said, and, rising, he came around to open the door for her. As they walked into the passageway she was relieved to see a trace of a smile on his lips as he murmured, 'And after Peter Frost I hope you've allowed yourself time for a cup of tea before all those late extras come flooding into your surgery to tax your energy to its limit.'

CHAPTER FOUR

Bearing in mind Ben's comment, Kate saw to it that she found time to eat a light snack before commencing her afternoon surgery. She wasn't sorry to have done so as at ten minutes past six the first of a stream of late arrivals arrived in Reception.

Kate's first patient was a child of three whose cough was a constant rasp. Kate diagnosed this as croup, the type of cough that would be relieved by breathing in moist air. Once reassured, the worried mother returned home with her young daughter, intending to make use of a simple remedy—a bathroom humidifier.

Kate's next patient was a man who'd caught his hand in a lawnmower. Although the sharp blades had narrowly missed severing his fingers, his thumb had been fractured. Explaining that the injury would require X-rays, Kate referred him to hospital, and by the time a friend had been summoned to drive him there another two casualties had arrived on the scene.

Lesley passed Kate their notes, lifting her eyebrows as she did so. 'These two young ladies have sunburn,' she explained ruefully, 'and one of them thinks she's been stung.'

Kate grinned and nodded as one young teenager hobbled into her room, her elbow supported by her friend. They had, it appeared, spent the day at the outdoor swimming pool. Both being fair-skinned, they'd burned to a lobster red in the hot lunchtime sun.

'A wasp stung me, too,' the wounded one complained, looking very sorry for herself as she sank into a chair. Kate came around to inspect her swollen ankle. 'Some ice cream dripped on my leg and I think the wasp got stuck in it. It's really ever so painful.'

At once Kate discovered the sting, still trapped under the surface of the blistered skin. Using tweezers, she gently plucked away the tiny barb, careful to avoid releasing the contents of the venom sac into the wound.

With her young patient vowing never to eat ice cream again, Kate recommended the generous use of calamine for both girls' sunburn and paracetamol for their discomfort which, she told them, would be greatest that night when they tried to find a comfortable position in bed.

After they'd gone Kate glanced at her watch and was startled to discover it was almost seven forty-five. By the time she left the surgery it was well past eight and when she arrived home she was, as Ben had warned her, feeling the tiring effects of the extra-long day.

That night, almost past the point of tiredness, Kate reflected on the important task ahead of her the next day—her apology to Hilly first thing in the morning. As she set her alarm and lifted her weary legs into bed she decided that a discreet peace offering would not go amiss.

So it was bright and early the next morning that Kate arrived at the florist and selected a posy of freesias. Presenting them to Hilly ten minutes later, she was relieved to see the young receptionist smile and knew that her apology had been accepted.

This hurdle safely over, Kate reflected there was one more yet to go—Peter Frost's appointment—and it was with some surprise that she found an unexpected ally in Peter's aunt, Mrs Mowbray. Having until now coped alone with her nephew's baffling troubles, she welcomed the attention of two doctors, despite the fact she'd had to rush away from work to attend the appointment.

On his examination Ben detected a slightly rapid pulse. Peter flinched as he palpated the tender quadricep muscles, and this, together with Peter's own version of his complaint coupled with his aunt's rendition, caused Kate to feel that she'd been correct in her suspicion

77

that Peter was a victim of ME.

However, when they'd gone Ben's tone was guarded as he rubbed his chin and frowned at Kate. 'I'll agree that Peter's symptoms meet the criteria for ME,' he murmured thoughtfully. 'Exercise-induced fatigue, neurological disturbances and limb tenderness —yes, that all adds up but, then, of course, he may simply be going through puberty and that affects some youngsters more disturbingly than others.'

'But surely,' Kate protested, 'the tiredness in itself isn't normal, even for puberty?'

'No, but he has seen a child psychologist and his findings are that the effect of the family split could have far-reaching consequences for Peter.'

Kate's disappointment increased as she saw she was going to receive no immediate support. 'Which confirms my inclination to have a full blood count and ESR done for Peter,' she decided firmly, 'as well as a check for auto-antibodies and MRI or SPET scans.'

Ben was silent for a moment, then he placed the notes back on her desk, his gaze coming up to meet hers. 'I take it you're convinced that Peter's symptoms warrant this depth of investigation?'

She nodded. 'Yes, I am.'

To her surprise he raised his shoulders in a brief shrug. 'All right, then, go ahead and let's see what kind of results we have there.' He walked slowly across the room towards the door but then, turning, he frowned at her. 'Oh, by the way, has Maureen told you we've decided on the date of Glyn's leaving party—the second Saturday in June?'

'No, she hasn't,' Kate answered, taken aback by the sharp change of subject.

'I was planning to hold it at the house,' he went on swiftly. 'In the garden if the weather holds.' He added quickly, as though he'd just remembered, 'Oh, and one more thing. The boys were intent on coming across when they saw your car arriving in the drive last night, but it was late and I thought the last thing you'd want was a knock at your door. I think they must be up to something so don't let them pester you.'

Kate smiled. 'Thank you for the warning.'

'You have my full permission to send them packing,' he added with a chuckle, and she laughed softly, relieved that the tension between them had eased.

Rising from the desk, she accompanied him out to Reception, where Damian was talking to Maureen Day.

'Ah, the lovely Kate!' Damian's voice carried clearly across the small area, causing several heads to turn. He strode towards Kate and took hold of her arm. 'How does a post-work reviver at the Red Lion strike you?' he asked loudly, making no effort to lower his voice.

It was hard to be cross with him, Kate

79

reflected as he teasingly resurrected the old warning of 'all work and no play makes Kate a dull girl'. As she politely declined she wished that he could be just a little more discreet in his flamboyant behaviour which, though harmless, could always set idle tongues wagging.

It was some time later when she sat down at her desk and thought how much Damian's exuberance reminded her of Julian. A small smile crossed her lips as hard on the heels of this discovery came the thought that she was now able to see the situation objectively, and she wondered how it had been possible that such smooth charm and superficial appeal could ever have attracted her, as had been the case with Julian.

Suddenly she realised that Jocylyn had entered her room and was staring at her curiously. Kate recovered herself and answered the queries put before her. However, she had the uncomfortable feeling that, despite her own amusement at the situation, Damian's attentions had not gone unnoticed and would doubtless be monitored in the future by the ever-perceptive staff.

*   *   *

To Kate's surprise, on Friday evening, her last patient was gone by six-thirty. Knowing that she was on call from Saturday onwards, she welcomed the early finish. She picked up her pager from her desk and slid it into her pocket, deciding that she now had time to fill her depleted kitchen cupboards.

Ten minutes later she arrived at the supermarket only to be horrified by the queues of late-night shoppers. She decided to settle for a sandwich instead and possibly spend some time with the twins. She drove out of the car park and, without stopping, made her way to Deer Lane.

As she was about to turn the car into the drive a vehicle blocked her path and she waited so that it could turn into the road. It was only when it emerged fully from behind the laurel that she saw it was the Land Rover and that Tom and Toby were sitting in the rear seats. Mary Graham was concentrating on the road, but as the two vehicles passed she met Kate's gaze, before speeding off.

Kate drove in and parked beside the Mercedes. The effect of the brief meeting with Mary Graham left Kate feeling slightly ill at ease as she tried to gather her thoughts. That incident, together with the fact she'd hurried home to see the twins and now there was no particular rush, left her wondering if she should head back to the supermarket and make the effort of shopping. Just as she was about to start the car engine again, Ben appeared, strolling around from the side of the house, his hands thrust in his pockets. He looked relaxed and casual, dressed in a green, collarless shirt and light summer trousers.

'Hi!' he greeted her as he opened her door. 'You've just missed the boys. A family friend called and offered them a test drive in a new Land Rover—I'm afraid it was too good an opportunity to miss.'

Kate climbed out, deciding to take a rain check on the shopping and opt for a long, slow soak in a herbal bath. 'Yes, I saw them,' she said casually, and smiled. 'Never mind, I expect I'll bump into them tomorrow.'

Ben shrugged. 'Can I tempt you to a glass of chilled wine on the tenace? The sun has just come around from the trees and we could sit in peace for half an hour before they return.'

Kate declined, explaining that she was eager to shower and eat. She beat a hasty retreat, only to feel annoyed with herself as she stood alone in her small sitting room and gazed out on the beautiful summer's evening, well aware of the fact she could now be sitting on the terrace enjoying a relaxing drink.

For the first time in months she felt a shadow of fatigue. She'd been so confident that the ME had finally passed and that she could look with confidence to the future, but as she sank to the sofa she realised this wasn't the physical fatigue of illness but weary disappointment, which had come over her when she'd passed the Land Rover a few minutes ago.

Kate framed Mary Graham's face in her mind—dark, sultry eyes and small features, lustrous hair and a confident smile. Taking a breath to alleviate the bewildering ache at her ribs, Kate kicked off her shoes and began to peel off her clothes. Five minutes later she was lying in a foamy bath, hoping the relaxing water would soothe away her unreasonable mood.

*   *   *

Kate's on-call duties over the weekend kept her busy. The majority of house calls were to patients suffering from stomach upsets, for which there was little she could do other than recommend rest, kaolin and morphine and plenty of fluids.

The boys finally called on her on Monday evening to ask her if she'd act as umpire for the games of tennis they'd planned for the children who were coming to Glyn Withycombe's party. Agreeing to their request, Kate then asked if they'd enjoyed their trip in the Land Rover and was rewarded by a full description of the excursion by Tom.

'Dr Graham used to be married,' Toby added, when his brother took a breath, 'but she got divorced from her husband about a year ago—'

'And we think she fancies Dad,' Tom interrupted with a cheeky grin.

Afraid her interest must be evident, Kate swiftly changed the subject, careful to avoid any more topics that concerned their father's friends. Though her curiosity had been aroused rather than quenched by the boys' remarks, she determined to spend the rest of the week concentrating solely on her work, a far safer topic than Ben's love life.

On Thursday, Sheila Dobson's symptoms caught her attention again. 'The chiropodist said nothing's wrong with my feet,' Sheila sighed, obviously exasperated. 'I just need bigger shoes, that's all, but I don't understand it. Look at my hands! I've had to have my wedding ring cut off because it was cutting into me. My fingers seemed to have grown, too.'

Kate examined them, but her fingers, though large with bulbous knuckles, appeared normal. 'And have your headaches improved?' Kate was curious to know if the new spectacles had helped.

Sheila shook her head. 'No, I still get them quite badly. If anything, they're worse.'

It was this remark that prompted Kate, more concerned with the headache problem than her patient's apparent growth of hands and feet, to decide on a CT scan, despite Sheila's dry protest that her brain was the one thing that didn't seem to have altered size. Later that day in the staff-room Kate found herself discussing the case with Ben.

'I rather think Sheila Dobson may have acromegaly,' she remarked as she sipped her coffee. The disease was caused by excessive secretion of growth hormone from the anterior pituitary gland.

Ben's eyebrows rose. 'That's unusual!'

Kate nodded. 'I've seen it once before—in training. The sufferer was male, but the physical appearance is very similar in both sexes—enlargement of hands and feet and a noticeable pronouncement of jaw.'

'Have you discussed this with her?' he asked.

Kate hesitated. 'No, not yet. The scan, after all, might not reveal a tumour, benign or otherwise.'

It was then that Brenda Tyler, the health visitor, who had been talking to Maureen Day, walked over and interrupted their conversation. 'Dr Buchan, I wonder if I could speak to you for a few moments about a nursing-home placement for an elderly patient?' she asked, pointing to her records which were spread open on the worktop.

'Yes, of course.' Ben nodded and, before turning to follow her, smiled at Kate. 'I'll apologise in advance for any disruption or noise coming from the house tomorrow. I'm afraid the boys and I will be starting the preparations for the party rather early.'

'Is there anything I can do to help?' Kate asked, before she'd given the matter any thought then suddenly realised that Ben might well have other help organised, specifically in the attractive shape and form of Mary Graham. Rather to her surprise, he accepted immediately.

'But I don't want to monopolise your whole Saturday,' he added, as an afterthought.

Kate shrugged. 'Oh, it's no trouble. As elected umpire of the junior tennis matches, I think I have to inspect the court anyway.'

They laughed and Kate watched him turn away to stride across to study the health visitor's large patient file.

She finished her drink and, before leaving, paused to talk with one or two of the other members of staff. As she walked downstairs she found herself thinking about the somewhat rash offer of help she'd made and the way Ben had seemed to accept it so readily. Perhaps Mary Graham was on duty at her own practice that morning or perhaps she had a prior appointment. There were any number of possible reasons, Kate decided. Almost in the next instant she found herself debating what she might wear to the party and whether or not it would be an appropriate occasion to wear the new blue dress that she'd recently bought.

She also realised it was a long time since she'd looked forward to a social occasion so much, which, she reflected ruefully, must say something about the quality of her social life! Walking into the silence of her room, she sighed and leaned back on the cool wood. She decided she'd wear the blue dress and, furthermore, she'd open an expensive box of perfume which had lain, unused, in her drawer for far too long.

*   *   *

On Saturday morning the sun shone hazily from a fine, pale mist, a sure sign of hot weather. Kate drew the blinds and pushed open the windows of the flat, aware that her sense of excitement was steadily increasing.

She wasn't surprised to hear the sounds of hammering and banging at just gone eight o'clock, and had only just finished dressing in shorts and sun top when Toby knocked on her door and asked if she had any navy cotton thread with which he could darn a split in his jeans.

Ten minutes later Kate was repairing the damage on her sewing machine and Toby was sitting on the sofa in his shorts, watching her.

'The caterers are coming at ten,' he explained as Kate ran the machine expertly along the seam. 'Dad's putting the trestle tables under the gazebo for the food to go on. Mrs Howard's not back from her daughter's yet, though, so he's not sure where everything should go. Dad said you might be coming across to help . . .'

Kate nodded as she snipped the thread and

87

handed back his jeans. 'I'll just tidy in the kitchen and then I'll come across with you.'

'Great!' exclaimed Toby as he tugged on his jeans. 'Dad's not cool with food and stuff. He said Tom and me would have to do the sandwiches if he got in a mess.'

Kate laughed. 'In that case, I think we'd better make the kitchen the first stop.'

A short while later they were walking across the lawns. Kate was about to take the path to the front of the house when a young girl rode up the drive on a bicycle, followed by Tom, also on his bike.

'That's Lisa,' said Toby excitedly. 'She said she might be coming over this morning.' And with that he was gone, leaving Kate standing in the middle of the path. Hearing loud hammering from the rear of the house, Kate decided to retrace her steps and follow the path to the terrace.

When she arrived there Ben, dressed in shorts and T-shirt, was wrestling with a sheet of gazebo awning which he was trying to secure to a pole. 'Hi—' he began, just as the canvas crumpled over his head.

Hiding her amusement, Kate hurried over to raise the offending flap. 'Need any help?' she volunteered. Her eyes widened innocently. 'Or is this men's work only?'

He grinned, his grey eyes filled with humour as he unravelled himself. 'Not at all. The boys' enthusiasm seems to have waned.'

Kate nodded. 'They have a visitor—rather a good-looking one.'

Ben rolled his eyes. 'Lisa Charwood—a friend from the squash club. I'm afraid they're both rivals for the her affections.' He gestured to the gazebo. 'Look, do you think you could hold this in place for a few moments while I go inside the house and find some stronger twine to secure it?'

Kate placed her fingers around the material. At the same time he wound his other arm around her in order to place her second hand in the correct position. She took a shuddering breath at the pressure of his chest against her back, his arms resting lightly over hers.

'Are you sure you can manage?' he asked softly, his breath coming down on her neck.

'Yes . . . yes. You go ahead,' she replied, aware that he was gazing down at her. His eyes took in her long, softly bronzed legs, her shorts and sun top and her hair, drawn back from her face in a golden plait which hung down her spine and which somehow seemed to be curved into the shape of his body. Her heart raced as she looked up at him. 'It's OK, I've got a grip now.'

His eyes still didn't leave her and for one moment she thought he was about to take her into his arms properly, but then he turned and began to stride purposefully towards the house.

Kate dropped her forehead against the pole

and breathed out slowly. What had happened between them just then? Dreading the moment he reappeared, she tried to compose herself—her fingers seemed to shake as they tightened around the pole.

'Where's Dad?' said a breathless voice, and Kate jumped as Tom came speeding around the corner of the house.

'Indoors, Tom, finding some twine to tie down the gazebo,' she answered, managing to steady her voice.

He gave her a puzzled look, then dashed off to the house. Seconds later Ben came hurtling out, a ball of strong-looking string in his hand. 'Caterers have just phoned to say they're on their way, and no Mrs Howard,' he told her, looking desperate.

'Would you like me to see them in?' she offered. 'Perhaps I can sort out a few things before Mrs Howard appears on the scene.'

'I'd be grateful,' he said with a sigh, 'for anything you could do in that department. I'm afraid the kitchen's a mess.'

She grinned. 'Not to worry. If you could just take this . . .' She tilted her head towards the pole.

'Of course!' He leapt towards her and again, as he moved beside her, Kate felt a frisson of awareness run down her spine. She somehow managed to disentangle herself and hurried to the kitchen by way of the French windows. She tried to steady her racing pulse and cool her cheeks before the caterers walked in.

Polly Glyn arrived with her two teenage daughters, Anabelle and Linda, a few minutes later. Polly and Kate set out the buffet onto trays while the girls ferried out the paper serviettes, cutlery and disposable plates to the trestle tables.

Mrs Howard finally arrived back in a taxi, with flustered apologies for being late, the coach having been held up in a traffic jam. Kate insisted she sit down with a cup of tea and, seeing that the food had been organised, the older woman breathed a sigh of relief.

When the last touches had been made to the feast, Kate slipped back to The Den to change. The blue dress lay on her bed, a calf-length, sleeveless creation in soft aqua, its slender, wrap-over skirt giving it a daring elegance. Washing her hair, she brushed it until it shone and wound it into a golden knot on the top of her head. As her hair, arranged like this, always added to her height, she chose to wear dainty silver thongs, which would feel cool and comfortable in the heat as well as look sophisticated. Her soft summer tan highlighted her fair eyebrows and her blue eyes were enhanced by the colour of her dress.

Kate studied her reflection in the mirror. Hesitating briefly, she added small blue stars to the lobes of her ears to give the last sparkling touch. Just as she was about to depart she heard a knock on the door downstairs.

Toby grinned shyly at her as she opened the door. He looked scrubbed and clean in fresh jeans and white T-shirt. 'I thought I'd call for you.' He shrugged. 'Everyone's arrived.'

As Kate accompanied Toby across the lawn, music spilled from the speakers Ben had erected over the terrace. People stood in little groups, talking animatedly as the sun shone down warmly, the final ingredient to make the perfect day for a party.

Kate waved to Angie, who hurried towards her. Toby disappeared with Phillip and Miriam to find the racquets for their game of tennis.

'You look gorgeous!' Angie studied Kate's dress. 'Is it new?'

'Oh, just a little bargain I picked up!' Kate grinned mischievously and they laughed.

As they strolled in the sunshine, Kate nodded to the group of people under the gazebo. 'Who's that pretty girl over there with Rupert?'

'Oh, that's Tessa Chandler,' Angie explained, frowning at the young redhead. 'She's Rupert's girlfriend—or rather fiancée. I think she works in London and doesn't manage to get down here very frequently. They became engaged at Christmas.'

'When is the big day?' Kate asked.

'October—so Maureen told me. They make a lovely couple, don't they?' Angie suddenly nudged Kate's arm. 'Look over there—do you see what I see?'

Kate followed Angie's gaze, her eyes coming to rest on Ben who was dressed in a smart, tan-coloured shirt and cream chinos. He stood talking to someone, who for the moment was obscured by a group of people moving across the lawn. When they'd passed, Kate found herself looking directly at Ben's attractive companion. Mary Graham was attired in figure-hugging white trousers and a white silk sun top with thin straps that lay demurely across her bare shoulders.

'Dr Mary Graham,' said Angie, echoing Kate's thoughts. 'The woman I told you about.'

Kate nodded slowly. 'Yes . . . she's lovely, isn't she?'

'It's pretty obvious she's crazy about Ben. You only have to look at them together. But . . .' Angie bit down on her lip and frowned. 'If you ask me, she won't make much headway unless she pops the question. How can anyone, even someone as pretty as Mary, compete with the memory of a perfect wife?' At Kate's slightly bemused expression, Angie added, 'After all, why else would a man stay so determinedly single for seven years? I think he's still wrapped up in the past.'

Kate had no answer to that, and for a moment she stood watching Ben and Mary Graham, wondering if what Angie had said was true. The boys, like Angie, had revealed that there was no lack of enthusiasm on Mary's part, and Ben certainly seemed to be enjoying her company at this moment, laughing and talking in an unusually relaxed fashion. Yet was Angie right? Could no other woman ever replace Paula in his affections?

Kate was startled from her reverie as the twins and Angie's children came running over, waving their tennis racquets. She was soon coaxed away to find herself on the tennis court, acting as umpire and trying, along with Linda and Anabelle's help, to referee a rather chaotic knock-about.

An energetic hour later she collapsed into a chair on the lawn as Glyn gave his poignant farewell speech. As she sat there her mind returned to what Angie had said of Paula, finally drawing the conclusion that Angie's candid observations were probably close to the truth.

When the party showed signs of breaking up, Kate helped Mrs Howard with clearing up. The Withycombes departed, and it was close to six when Kate found herself alone in the kitchen, filling the dishwasher.

'Sorry, but the washing-up seems to be endless,' Ben apologised as he appeared beside her, about to lower a tray of china to the worktop. Surprisingly, he was alone and not accompanied by Mary. Kate had imagined she'd remain after the party had broken up.

'Everyone's gone, except Rupert and his

girlfriend,' he told her, surprising her further. Involuntarily, she turned to stare at him. 'So this should be amongst the last of the debris.' He hovered uncertainly, the tray looking perilously like overbalancing as he tried to squeeze it onto a few spare inches of worktop.

'Here let me—' Kate began, barely recovering from the surprise that Mary Graham, it appeared, had left. She reached out, intending to take some of the plates, but as their fingers brushed she jumped at the electricity that seemed to spark between them. Glancing up into his eyes, she felt her stomach tighten as the tray clattered noisily to the worktop.

Almost as though they were moving in slow motion, he reached out and gently drew her into his arms. She went unresistingly, shuddering as his hands slid around her waist and drew her slender body against him. Without a word he bent to kiss her, a soft and fleeting kiss—a hesitant, tender enquiry. Her fingers, finding a life of their own, slid to his shoulders and brushed the smooth, thick, dark hair at his nape. At this he pulled her against him, his mouth returning to crush her lips with an intensity that sent her heart crashing against her ribs.

'Kate . . . ?' he murmured huskily, his fingers coming up to smooth her cheek in soft, tender strokes. 'Kate, I—'

At that moment there were footsteps in the

hall and Kate jumped, the blood pounding in her head as she moved away just seconds before Mrs Howard's bustling figure came hurrying through the doorway.

CHAPTER FIVE

The telephone rang at half past ten that evening when Kate was on the point of going to bed. She hadn't undressed but had let her hair down, sliding the pins from the knot and brushing it free.

'It's me,' said Ben as she lifted the receiver. 'Were you in bed?'

'No, not yet,' she said hesitantly.

'Would you mind if I came over briefly? I promise I shan't keep you long.'

Since the moment Mrs Howard had almost discovered them in the kitchen there had been no opportunity to talk as Rupert had remained to help with the dismantling of the gazebo.

Kate had helped Mrs Howard, who seemed not to have noticed the strained silence in the kitchen when she'd come in. Concerned that the older woman looked rather tired, Kate had offered to finish the last of the clearing away. Once this had been done Kate had slipped quietly back to The Den, while Ben and Rupert worked in the garden.

Kate's pulse began to race as she agreed to

96

see him, saying she'd come downstairs and unlock the door. She only had time to glance quickly around her sitting room, plump up the cushions on the sofa and compose her scattered train of thought. Then, hurrying downstairs, she slid the lock on the door just as Ben's tall figure materialised out of the darkness. He was still dressed in the tan shirt and chinos he had worn that afternoon, and his eyes met hers uncertainly.

'I'm sorry it's so late,' he apologised as she closed the door.

She returned his smile and led the way upstairs. Without speaking, he crossed the room to the window, where for a few moments he stood gazing out into the night. Finally he turned and, sitting on the sofa, thrust his large hand through his hair.

'Would you like some coffee or a drink of some sort?' she offered uncertainly.

'Actually, I don't think I can face any more drink or food today, thanks all the same,' he said with a smile. His gaze lingered on her hair which fell around her shoulders, gleaming in the soft light. 'Come and sit down,' he said quietly. 'I need to talk to you.' He held out his hand and for a moment her heart thumped wildly against her chest. She walked to the sofa and slid her fingers into his, sinking into the cushions beside him.

'Firstly,' he murmured on a deep sigh, 'I haven't thanked you properly for all you did

97

for us today. Goodness knows what would have happened to the buffet if you hadn't been there to organise it. The whole lot would have remained in the kitchen and still under Cellophane by the time everyone arrived, I expect.'

'I enjoyed today,' she murmured, conscious of the way her hand rested in his. Had he kissed her on the spur of the moment and had now come to tell her he regretted it? Kate tried to read his eyes. In spite of the fact that she herself wasn't ready for any kind of deep romantic involvement, she had, nevertheless, responded to his kiss, and it would be less than honest if she tried to deny the strong attraction she felt towards him.

He was smiling at her as though he could read her thoughts. 'And the second thing is,' he went on, 'I must apologise for my behaviour in the kitchen. Heaven alone knows, I hadn't planned it . . . May I take it I'm forgiven?'

'For what?' She looked into his eyes and smiled.

One hand lifted to push gently through her hair. 'You look beautiful tonight, Kate. So lovely.'

For a moment time seemed to stand still as she lost herself in his gaze, feeling the soft, sensual touch of his fingers brush against her neck. Then he leaned back into the cushions and closed his eyes for a few seconds before opening them again. 'Suddenly I find I don't want to leave here,' he murmured in a husky whisper, and they exchanged tentative, awkward smiles.

'Where do the boys think you are?' she asked curiously.

He grinned. 'They collapsed in bed about ten, absolutely shattered.'

'You must be very proud of them at times like today,' she said quietly.

He nodded. 'Yes, I am.' With a shrug he added, 'Sometimes I have my doubts, though. Toby is going through a rough patch at school. I feel I either overcompensate for Paula or I'm not firm enough.' He smiled wryly. 'I remember only too well what it was like with my brother and I. Miles is a year older than me, and we needed a firm hand. But it doesn't make me feel any better when I try to employ the same standards. Sometimes I really do think they miss a woman's touch.' He paused. 'Toby told me your parents died in an accident, too.'

Kate nodded. 'A car crash, when I was five.'

'That was tough.' He shook his head slowly.

'As a matter of fact, I've always thought how fortunate I was. I had two sets of parents instead of one, and when my adoptive mother died when I was ten I really missed her, perhaps even more than my own mother, because I had so many happy memories.'

He frowned thoughtfully. 'And your adoptive father?'

Kate hesitated. 'I was lucky there, too. Dad lived long enough to see me qualify. He was in his eighties when he had a massive stroke. Luckily, Julian and I didn't split up until after his death . . . that would have upset him dreadfully.'

'Julian?'

'My fiancé.' She made a conscious effort to relax her fingers, still lying in his. 'I'm afraid we . . .' She found herself lost for words and settled for the most innocuous. 'Well, we just seemed to drift apart. I think my ME was probably the biggest factor.'

'I would have thought you needed his support more than ever then,' Ben murmured as he brushed his thumb against the soft skin of her wrist.

Kate paused, knowing how much it would have meant to her if Julian had helped her through the illness, but she understood that for some people illness was anathema. She shrugged. 'Julian had a career as a high-profile lawyer. He was going places and I just seemed to lag behind all the time. Illness and that kind of ambition in a relationship just doesn't mix.'

'I'm sorry, Kate.'

'It's a long time ago now. And we move on, don't we? At least it's given me the opportunity to do some things I thought I never would.'

He looked at her curiously. 'Such as?'

'Well, moving to the Dales, for instance.'

100

She felt her face warm as she remembered the heated discussions she'd had with Julian over their future. 'I've always been attracted to the countryside. Julian would never have left London . . .' She looked at Ben for a moment, realising she seemed to be talking rather a lot about herself. 'What about you? Have you never thought of remarrying?' she asked hesitantly.

He lifted his dark eyebrows. 'No, I can't say that I have. After Paula I didn't want any kind of deep involvement—all I could think about was making life as secure as I could for the boys. They were old enough to remember Paula, and I suppose I wanted to try to preserve what memories they had—avoid any possibility of disappointment for them in the future.'

He said this expressionlessly, but Kate sensed a deep hurt lying behind the words as well as the rock-solid determination that fired his obvious determination to shield his boys. 'But wasn't that hard for you, bringing up two young children and having work to cope with?' she found herself asking.

He was silent for a moment. 'Raising the boys on my own was a conscious decision I made—and I haven't regretted it. Before coming to Milchester I did consider moving south, where my parents live. But I knew they had their own lives to lead, as we did, though we keep in contact regularly, just as we do with

Paula's parents who live in America.'

They sat in silence again, and Kate shuddered as he drew his fingers between hers. A strange sensation fluttered inside her, like a small bird trapped below her ribs. Then he moved towards her. She sensed that what had happened in the kitchen was about to happen again, and she also knew there was nothing she could do to prevent it.

He pulled her into his arms and kissed her, her body responding to his powerful grip and the way his lips moved over hers. Warm and firm, but not intrusive, they teased a gentle pattern over the sensitive contours of her mouth, giving her ample opportunity to pull away. But she didn't.

Instead, she leaned into him, and with a soft groan of desire he pulled her harder against him and kissed her with a force that made her give a startled gasp. 'Oh, Kate,' he murmured against her lips, 'you're so lovely . . . so warm . . . I hadn't intended this either.'

Catching her breath, she stared up at him. 'I don't suppose either of us did, Ben.'

Kate realised as she said this how easy it would be to fall for someone like him, a man who seemed so rooted and assured in his own world—a world which would be virtually impossible for any woman to penetrate. The thought of Mary Graham flashed through her mind and Kate wondered again at the puzzling relationship they seemed to share. Was it because of Ben's determined resolve not to be committed that the lovely young doctor was not at this moment by his side?

However, as her mind roved, her eyes seemed to be locked into the silvery depths that glittered only inches away and her heart beat a tattoo that pulsated into her throat. As if he realised the effect he was having on her he released her slightly, shaking his head. 'Damn it, Kate, I don't seem to be able to stop myself where you're concerned. I told myself I just needed to come across and apologise for what happened today, but here I am, finding it impossible not to touch you . . . kiss you . . .'

This time they kissed with an equal intensity, a mutual desire that made Kate shake inside. His hands moved over her breasts and she arched against him, knowing that whatever was happening between them she wasn't able to stop it. Another convulsive shudder went through her as she caught his expression and he sighed.

'Oh, Kate, I want you. You know that, don't you?' Before she could answer he clasped her head between his large palms and brought her mouth to his lips in a passionate kiss that left her breathless. Her fingers seemed to link of their own accord around his neck and she heard her own ragged breathing, felt the long-forgotten surge of craving inside her.

As he fought to find the zip at the back of her dress, she arched against him as his dark hair brushed sensually against her cheek. A shudder ran through him and seemed to enter her body too. Suddenly he was staring at her, imprisoning her wrists, his breath coming in shallow gasps as he gazed at her with hungry eyes.

'Kate . . . this is crazy!'

'I know,' she whispered. 'I know.'

'And tomorrow morning?' he said raggedly. 'What happens then? When we have to face what we've done?' His grip on her wrists relaxed and he drew her into his arms, pinning her there as though to stop both of them from moving. The gesture emphasised the control he was asserting in order to restrain his desire.

She closed her eyes and inhaled his earthy aroma and knew that everything about him made her physically aware of his presence. She wanted him to make love to her. For the first time since Julian she seemed to have come alive. But she also knew he was right— tomorrow they would probably both be sorry for something done so recklessly on the spur of the moment. She eased herself gently away from his chest, and slowly he let her go.

'We're both tired,' he said, and she nodded.

Pushing himself up from the sofa, he looked down at her, an expression of regret on his face as he met her confused eyes. 'Damn it, Kate. Believe me, there's nothing I want more at this moment than to stay . . .'

She stood up, her legs shaky, and smoothed

down the crumpled layers of her dress. 'I think it's better if you go,' she managed to say.

'Let's start again from tomorrow.' He reached out to touch her hair, his fingers lingering for a few moments on its silky surface. 'One day at a time . . . yes?'

She nodded.

He gave her a weary smile and walked to the door. Turning back briefly, he whispered uncertainly, 'Kate . . . ?' For a few seconds her heart thudded expectantly in her chest, but before she was able to answer he spoke. 'Don't come downstairs. I'll see myself out. Sweet dreams.'

She felt sure it wasn't what he'd been about to say but she merely nodded. 'You, too, Ben.'

She heard the click of the latch downstairs, and she sank onto the sofa, not believing she could feel such a sense of dismay. How close had they come to making love just then? And her body was still aching for him, yearning for the touch and caress of his fingers which had brought her body to such a pitch of awareness.

Yet he'd made it plain that he was content with his life, that he had no yearning to change the pattern of his existence. Not even, it appeared, for someone like Mary Graham.

Kate knew that if she were sensible she'd forget about what had happened today and attempt to view the remainder of her time in Milchester as an opportunity to broaden her career and steer clear of emotional tangles.

If she were sensible . . .

*   *   *

Kate was on call the following day, Sunday.

The house was quiet when she went to unlock her car at mid-morning and the Mercedes wasn't parked in its usual spot. Deciding Ben must have taken the boys out, she completed her first call to an asthmatic, then was summoned immediately to another. Two more calls to patients with viral symptoms and a crisis at a local nursing home which involved one of her elderly patients meant that she didn't return home until late afternoon. The car was still absent and the house silent.

That night she thought she heard the boys playing tennis, but when she was called out at ten past eleven to yet another case of high temperature and sickness the house was in darkness.

On Monday she left home earlier than usual, not wanting to bump into Ben before surgery. She wanted time and space to compose herself before she met him. The surgery was packed, she discovered. The viral epidemic was spreading.

Matters weren't helped by Rupert being on holiday and the absence of Bal Chandra, another victim of the virus. That left Meg James, Ben and Kate to manage the surgeries, and it wasn't until someone fainted in

106

Reception that Kate found herself at Ben's shoulder, attempting to help their patient back to her seat.

'It's so warm in here,' muttered the patient, as Kate put a glass to her lips.

'Perhaps five minutes in the fresh air,' Ben suggested, and smiled at Kate, their eyes meeting briefly across the woman's head.

Kate returned his smile. The warmth in his eyes made her feel oddly light-headed and strangely excited, and to cover her confusion she offered to accompany their recovering patient to the garden. She felt that she was in need of air herself!

It wasn't until the following day that she saw him again. Reception was besieged with patient queries. They acknowledged each other's presence with tired smiles, then turned back to address the problems of the twenty-odd impatient faces awaiting attention in the waiting area.

Toby was a daily visitor to The Den that week, coming over from the house after school and watching her small portable television or playing her CDs. She grew to look forward to the hour or so he passed with her and the topics they discussed. Sometimes they talked about school and sometimes about his friends, like Peter Frost. They also often talked about Tom and Lisa who seemed now to be more Tom's companion than Toby's.

'What does your father think about Tom

and Lisa going out together?' Kate asked one day, wondering if Ben was really keeping out of her way or whether she was becoming paranoid.

'Dunno,' muttered Toby. 'Haven't seen him much.' He squatted on Kate's leather pouffe, moving a tiny clay figure skilfully over Kate's chessboard.

'I'm afraid it's frantic at the surgery,' Kate murmured by way of explanation as she tried in vain to save her king from checkmate.

'What's new?' Toby muttered grimly. 'It always is.'

Kate glanced up in surprise, shocked at his tone. Did he really feel as resentful as he sounded? Or was she reading too much into it?

It was a perfect summer's morning when Kate next saw Ben. She had just locked the flat door and was heading for the Volkswagen when he turned the corner of the house and waved.

'You're early,' he called cheerfully as she approached.

'And you're late,' she teased, her heart beating rapidly as he laid one long brown arm on the roof of the car behind her. Automatically her hand went up to smooth her hair, and she felt ridiculously self-conscious as his gaze lingered on her face then followed her flustered fingers along their shaky path.

'Tell me, why do you always wear it up?' he

asked, a curious smile playing at his lips.

'My hair?' She dropped her hand quickly from the neat golden knot. 'Well, it's tidy and cool, I suppose.' She shrugged. 'That's rather a leading question for this time of the morning. I haven't woken up yet.'

'I like it better down—free, flowing over your shoulders.' His grey eyes held a spark of amusement at her obvious confusion. 'As it was after Glyn's party, when you'd taken out all the bits and pieces and you still had on that beautiful dress . . .'

She felt her face grow crimson. 'It seems ages ago now.'

He nodded. 'Too long. Far too long.'

He looked at her with silvery grey eyes that seemed to burn through her. She met his gaze and saw the message written clearly there.

'Kate . . .' He moved towards her and was about to take her hand when she saw a movement from the house. Mrs Howard was shaking a duster from the top window. Kate stepped back quickly.

'Isn't Rupert back today?' she asked quickly, to cover her embarrassment, and he gave her a deep, confused frown.

Sensing her recoil, he nodded. 'Yes, with luck we'll all be back to normal.'

Kate smiled. 'Toby will be pleased.'

'Oh, why's that?' He looked at her curiously.

'Just that I think he's looking forward to seeing your parents. He told me you were taking them on holiday soon.'

His face cleared. 'Yes. Indeed I am.' He straightened his shoulders as the awkward silence between them seemed to deepen, and then, before he opened his car door, he said haltingly, 'I wonder . . . On Friday I'm making a house call to Hugh Conway and I see that you have a visit marked down for Sarah. Perhaps we could drive out together. It makes sense, really, as far as transport goes.'

Kate couldn't help but smile. 'Yes, that's true.'

'So . . . see you then?'

She nodded, and as he disappeared into the Mercedes he gave her a grin, accompanied by a toot of the horn. Kate eventually slid in to the Volkswagen and sat there for a few seconds, her heart pounding in her chest. Looking into the driver's mirror, she saw the sparkling eyes of a stranger.

With a start, she realised they were her own.

*   *   *

On Friday the temperature leapt. The meteorological office gave predictions of record highs and the news bulletins warned of severe road congestion, with holiday traffic building up for the weekend.

Kate's early surgery was, not surprisingly, brimming with casualties. Sunburn, insect bites, stings and nose-bleeds seemed to be most prevalent. Though they were all minor ailments, at eleven-thirty she welcomed the cup of coffee Hilly brought her.

'Dr Buchan would like to know if you want to accompany him on a house visit when your surgery is over,' Hilly remarked, frowning down at her notepad. 'It's the Conways, Splinters Cottage, by the flyover. He says you know about it?'

'Yes, I do.' Kate paused, trying to swallow the erratic pulse that had suddenly leapt into her throat. 'Do we have any more information on Mrs Conway's impending laparoscopy?'

Hilly nodded. 'Do you want me to look in her notes?'

'No, don't bother at the moment. Just make sure I have all the paperwork when I leave.'

Hilly hesitated. 'So you and Dr Buchan will be travelling out . . . together?'

Kate looked up, keeping her expression blank. 'Er, yes. It seems sensible as we're making the same house call.'

Hilly nodded uncertainly. 'Oh, right, yes. So, if either of you are wanted, we can page you together?'

'Yes,' Kate answered without hesitation, and gave a casual shrug.

'Well, I'd better make a note in the book, then.' Hilly departed but Kate found it difficult to concentrate afterwards. The curious expression in the receptionist's eyes had said it all, and it annoyed Kate fleetingly to think that

111

she'd been forced to explain herself.

She finally retrieved her normal thought processes and saw several more patients, before clearing her desk by twelve. She risked hurrying through Reception to pay a quick visit to the cloakroom. Having checked her appearance—hair turned into a glossy chignon, a pale peach cotton shirt tucked into an ivory skirt with a narrow leather belt and elegant court shoes—she made her exit with a businesslike wave to the girls at the desk.

She found Ben waiting for her outside. He smiled, dressed smartly in a light linen jacket and dark trousers, his black hair smoothed back from his forehead. 'Made it at last,' he said with a sigh as they both climbed into the Mercedes.

'Was it a difficult morning?' Kate smoothed down her skirt as she relaxed into the comfortable leather seat, vaguely wondering if they were being observed from the office window.

He turned to cast her a wry grin. 'After Mrs Dalkenny I'm gasping for breath!'

Kate's eyebrows arched. She'd been at the surgery long enough to know that Mrs Dalkenny had achieved almost mythic status in the archives of the practice with her variety of illnesses.

'I persuaded her that malaria was probably not on the agenda in the Scilly Isles, even if she was bitten by a particularly loathsome mosquito while on holiday,' he said with a chuckle. 'And, even though I did have to cheat, it's wonderful to have an hour with you,' he added in a quiet, husky voice that made her heart leap.

The Mercedes quickly sped out from the town centre and onto the motorway, and for a moment he turned and their eyes met again. 'You know, what with Tom sneaking out of the house whenever he has the opportunity to see Lisa,' he remarked dryly, 'and Toby breezing across to see you every evening, I'm feeling decidedly redundant.'

Kate laughed softly. 'Well, you could always come across with Toby.'

He nodded. Then, as he looked back at the road, he said in a distracted voice, 'Toby's been rather withdrawn lately. Have you noticed?'

Kate didn't like to mention the conversation she'd had with Toby. 'Perhaps it's just a phase he's going through,' she suggested.

'So you *have* noticed?'

She knew she was bordering on dangerous territory. To try to advise any parents on their children was difficult, but her relationship with Ben was delicate—how could she just blunder in and say that she felt Toby was feeling neglected?

'Tom doesn't seem to be interested in hanging out with Toby lately,' he went on almost to himself. 'He seems to be too

113

involved with Lisa, and I'm wondering if that's having an effect.'

'Have you talked to Toby?' Kate asked. 'I mean lately?'

Ben frowned. 'There hasn't really been time for a heart-to-heart. And he's always reluctant to talk to me about school. He's never really settled at Milchester High, not like Tom.' Ben shrugged. 'Anyway, that's my problem. Not yours.'

Just as Kate was on the verge of saying she'd like to help if she could, the flyover came into sight and the Conways' cottage appeared beneath it. A few minutes later they were standing in front of the tiny oak door.

Sara welcomed them with her usual smile, though Kate saw at once that she looked very anxious and pale. Leaving Ben and Hugh together, Sara led Kate into the garden where they sat on a wooden bench, surrounded by Hugh's beautifully fragrant roses.

'I'm due to go for the laparoscopy next week,' Sara explained worriedly. 'I haven't told Hugh yet. He's seemed better recently and I decided I wouldn't say anything until closer to the time.'

'Are you back at work?' Kate asked.

'I haven't felt confident enough to leave Hugh. It's strange, but at this time of year he always seems to have a low period.'

Kate knew that the post-traumatic stress disorder from which Hugh Conway suffered was thought to have resulted from one of his military stints overseas, but there had never been any clear incident that Hugh recalled in therapy, which would have given an indication as to the original cause of his disease.

'Ben was the one to diagnose Hugh's PTSD,' Sara added quietly. 'It was about ten years ago when we lived in Surrey, where Hugh was stationed, and the Buchans had just returned from South Africa. Ben was one of the doctors of a group practice that Hugh attended. At the time Hugh was suffering from stomach pains, which the army doctor thought was an ulcer.'

'But it wasn't?' Kate said.

'No. He had various investigations until one day Ben persuaded him to talk about his feelings which, up until that point, Hugh had hidden. Ben finally put a name to what was going on—post-traumatic stress disorder. He persuaded Hugh to see a colleague for therapy and, thank God, the nightmares started to subside.'

'It must have been very worrying for you,' Kate sympathised.

'Well, it was only when Ben helped him to see he wasn't going crazy and he really was suffering from PTSD that the whole thing fell into place. I think that if Ben hadn't seen us through that time we wouldn't be together now.' Sara looked up and added slowly, 'We were devastated for him when Paula died.

After all that had happened, we thought there might have been time to . . .'

Kate sat quietly, her heart thudding as she waited for Sara to speak again, but before either of them could continue their conversation a series of loud bangs echoed across the peaceful garden, followed by an eerie silence.

'The motorway!' Sara gasped. 'It sounds like an accident.'

Both women sprang to their feet, ran back into the house and out to the front garden. Ben was already there, shading his eyes with hands, squinting up at the flyover. 'Can't see anything from here,' he shouted to Kate. 'Better drive up and take a look.'

In a matter of seconds they'd jumped into the Mercedes as Sara flew back into the cottage to phone the emergency services. Kate looked back through the rear window to see Hugh's ashen face as he stood staring up dazedly at the flyover.

By the time they arrived at the motorway a policeman was already diverting traffic. Ben slowed the Mercedes, winding down the window to explain that they were doctors.

Parking behind the police car on the hard shoulder, they were met by the stomach-turning sight of vehicles strewn across the road. 'If you take the white car,' Ben called as they scrambled out, 'I'll see to the one on the right.'

Kate nodded, but as she turned a policeman hailed her from the grass verge. She ran towards him and realised he was pointing to a red van which had careered down an embankment and into a tree.

Arriving at the vehicle, Kate took a breath as steam hissed fiercely from an almost unrecognisable engine. Glass was strewn everywhere and the driver, apparently the only occupant, had been propelled through the windscreen. He lay on his back some yards away from his vehicle.

Kate trod carefully over the glass and metal and knelt beside the young man to check for any sign of life, fighting an instinctive recoil of her stomach at the sight of the terrible injuries that signified he was probably beyond all help.

'No seat belt,' the policeman said with a sigh above her as she opened her case on the grass. 'When will they ever learn?'

Kate shook her head slowly as it became evident during her examination that the victim had died on impact. She finally climbed the verge again, relieved to hear the sound of wailing sirens. As ambulances and fire vehicles sped up to the scene, Kate hurried across to the white car.

'Driver's door's stuck,' explained another officer breathlessly, as he pulled at the passenger door. Kate peered in and saw that the driver was a young woman, her head slumped back against the headrest, obviously

117

unconscious.

'I'll crawl across,' she told the policeman, when he'd managed to prise open the door. Disregarding his warning and the splintered metal of the console which had fractured under the broken windscreen, she began to squeeze across the seat.

It was only when she felt for the pulse in the girl's outstretched arm that she saw blood pumping from her thigh. Kate carefully removed a shard of glass that lay on the wound over her blood-soaked jeans and which must have caused the injury. Quickly she removed her own shirt and folded it into a pad, applying direct pressure to slow down the blood loss. For a moment she froze. Under the tangle of blonde hair she recognised Tessa, Rupert's fiancée, whom she had last spoken to at Glyn's party.

When the fire crew had disconnected the twisted door from its hinges and peeled away the console from over the girl's legs Kate released her hold on the pressure pad, allowing one of the firemen to take over as she administered a pain-relieving injection of pethidine.

Trying to distance herself from the fact this was someone she knew, she gave instructions to the paramedics as they removed Tessa to the ambulance. With a pre-formed plastic collar stabilising her neck movement and saline replacing lost body fluids, Kate watched

Tessa's prone figure disappear into the ambulance.

It was only when she felt the soft cloth of a linen jacket go around her shoulders that she realised Ben had arrived beside her, his sleeves rolled up to his elbows and dirt covering the front of his shirt.

'Oh . . . thanks,' she murmured gratefully as she gripped the jacket. 'What happened to the occupants of the grey car?'

'There are two serious casualties,' he told her grimly, 'both with head and spinal injuries. The driver's in shock with no apparent physical injury.'

Kate hesitated, laying her fingers over his arm. 'Ben, the young woman in this ambulance is Tessa, Rupert's girlfriend.'

He drew in a breath as the ambulance doors shut. 'Tessa? Tessa Chandler? You're sure?'

Kate nodded. 'Yes, I'm afraid so.'

'How serious is it?'

Kate looked uncertain. 'She has a very bad leg wound and head injury and there is, of course, the possibility of internal bleeding.'

He nodded abruptly as the ambulance sped off. 'She must have been travelling back to London today. I'll ring Bal from the mobile— he's on duty at the surgery with Rupert.'

Kate accompanied Ben back to the Mercedes and sat beside him as he telephoned, waiting in silence as he passed on the news.

Moments later he sighed as he replaced the mobile. 'If Rupert decides to go to the hospital, I'll attend to the remainder of his calls. But I'm afraid there's even more bad news . . .' His profile hardened as he leaned forward to start the car. 'Toby's been in a fight at school.' With a heavy shrug he turned towards her. 'The head has suspended him.'

CHAPTER SIX

On the journey back to Milchester Ben was silent. Trying to think of how she could best help, Kate came up with few constructive answers.

'What are you going to do about Toby?' she asked after a while.

He shrugged. 'Naturally I want to know what happened at school, but Rupert's surgery begins at two. It's almost that now. I'll ring the headmaster and tell him I'll be along as soon as I can.'

Kate knew how she'd feel in Toby's shoes. Whatever he'd done—and she didn't believe for one moment that the boy deserved suspension simply for being in a fight—waiting for the arrival of his father would only add to his misery.

'I'm quite happy to take Rupert's patients while you collect Toby,' she said. Without removing his gaze from the road, he shook his head.

'Thanks all the same, but I'll see to it.'

Kate sighed quietly, unable to understand why he wouldn't accept this obvious solution, but she thought better of pressing the point and very soon they were back at surgery. Bal explained that he'd broken the news about Tessa, and Rupert had left for Milchester General. As Kate went to her room Lesley dashed across and pushed something wrapped in a Cellophane bag into her hands. 'It's a spare blouse I keep on hand for emergencies. You look as though you might need it.'

Kate glanced down at Ben's jacket. 'Oh, thanks, I'd forgotten . . . I dirtied my own top at the accident scene.' She asked hesitantly, 'How did Rupert take the news?'

Lesley shrugged. 'He didn't say very much, but he went as white as a sheet, poor lamb. We were all so shocked. Apparently, they'd had a fantastic holiday together, too.'

Kate sighed. 'Thanks for the blouse, Lesley.' Just as she turned away she heard Ben call across to explain he was about to change his clothes before surgery then he'd make a telephone call to Milchester High.

Kate couldn't help but think of Toby waiting anxiously at school. As she slid off the jacket to replace it with Lesley's blouse she saw no sense at all for Ben to take Rupert's list when she herself was free.

121

Sweeping up the jacket, she hurried out again and knocked on Ben's door. At his response she entered, noticing immediately that he'd already changed into a fresh white shirt and had combed his hair neatly back from his face. His hand lay on the telephone.

'What is it, Kate?' he asked abruptly, glancing at his jacket and nodding to the chair. 'Just leave it there, will you?'

Kate did so, then said firmly, 'May I speak to you before you make that call?'

He looked surprised, but to her dismay he merely cupped the receiver to his shoulder. His forehead furrowed.

'It's about Toby,' she began, taking a breath.

'I'm about to speak to the school,' he said, still frowning.

She paused. 'Won't you reconsider? I could quite easily take Rupert's surgery before my own, which would allow you time to collect Toby and talk to him.'

Finally replacing the telephone, he looked across at her and leaned back in his chair. 'Doubtless you mean well, Kate, but Toby's got himself into this trouble and he has only himself to blame. An hour or two to think it over won't do him any harm. As I've said, it's my responsibility to cover for Rupert and to see his patients are catered for—not yours.'

'By any chance,' she asked quietly, 'does your refusal to accept my help have anything to do with before—with those late extras?'

'Why should you think that?'

She shrugged. 'Perhaps you felt I was trying to interfere then—and you do now.'

He looked at her for a moment, a small, tight muscle beginning to work at the base of his jaw. 'Kate, this is nothing to do with us or with our professional differences. It's a separate—family—issue.' He hesitated. 'As I've said, since Toby started at Milchester High there's been a gap neither he nor I can seem to bridge. He can't just expect me to down tools at the drop of a hat. I have to try to deal with the situation in whichever way I think best.'

'Yes, but maybe today is the perfect opportunity to get closer to him.'

'What do you mean?' He frowned. 'I can't exactly *condone* a suspension.'

'I'm not suggesting you should. But give him a fair chance to explain. If he's kept hanging around at school, well, he'll know you've already passed judgement. But if you go now, take him home and let him see you're making time for him . . .'

He gave a sharp sigh. 'Time. I wish there was more of it.'

Kate nodded. 'I expect Toby does, too.'

'But I'm a GP, Kate. The boys have to understand that. Tom seems to.'

'Which is something Toby is probably confused about himself.' She flushed and looked at him under her lashes. 'Tom is pretty laid back about everything. He's well adjusted at school and interested in girls.' She shrugged. 'It must be pretty devastating to feel alienated from someone who has always been your other half. It must seem lonely and bewildering . . . Growing up is hard enough, without losing your best friend and your brother.'

It was a long time before Ben spoke or even moved, his eyes going slowly over her face. Finally, he pushed himself to his feet, walked around his chair to the window and then came back again. One large hand reached out for the telephone and he stabbed out a number. As he waited for a response his eyes came up to meet Kate's.

She managed not to wither under his gaze, her heart still doing acrobatics as the silence in the room deepened. Finally he looked away, giving his instructions in a clear voice.

'Change of plan,' he told Lesley in Reception. 'Dr Ross will be taking Dr Greaves's surgery this afternoon so will you let each patient know as they come in? Should there be any problems, rebook them for Rupert next week.'

When he'd replaced the phone he looked at Kate. 'I'll be back for this evening's session— hopefully.' He shot her a dark look, one eyebrow arched. 'OK?'

She nodded. 'Good luck.'

He swept his case under his arm and strode out of the door. The last she heard of him was his deep voice, calling goodbye to the girls on Reception. She expelled a long sigh, staring ahead of her. She hadn't expected that.

A few moments later she found herself at the desk, confirming Ben's instructions with the receptionists. She reflected that the next time she saw him she might not be feeling quite so smug about her victory.

* * *

Luckily, the first three of Rupert's patients had no qualms in seeing her, but the fourth was Denise Markham and Kate's spirits sank as she saw the woman enter, wondering if her real problems had only just begun.

'I've been told my doctor has been called away,' she said abruptly.

'Yes,' Kate confirmed. 'I'm sorry, but Dr Greaves had to leave on a matter of urgency and, rather than cancel his appointments, I'm taking surgery on his behalf.' She halted at her patient's refusal to be seated, reflecting that it had been Denise who'd made the complaint to Rupert about her refusal to give an antiviral to Sean and that the young woman was probably still feeling antagonistic towards her. 'I'm sure we can arrange an appointment soon if you would prefer to see him,' Kate added swiftly.

Denise Markham sighed. 'That's no use. I made this appointment because it's the only time I have without the kids.'

Kate gestured to the chair. 'In that case, please sit down. How are the boys?'

'All right,' muttered the young woman as she sat, making her discontent with seeing Kate patently clear.

'How may I help?' Kate asked, determined to avoid unpleasantness.

'You probably can't. Or won't,' was the flat reply.

'Mrs Markham,' Kate said evenly, taking a long breath, 'I'll try my best to help, but I think we should discontinue this consultation if you have reservations about seeing me.'

'I've reservations about seeing any doctor,' she snapped. 'What would you know about bringing up two kids, paying all the bills and keeping a roof over their heads? You doctors have fantastic salaries—you've no idea what some women on their own have to make do with.'

Kate glanced at the computer and saw no mention of Denise Markham being either divorced or separated. She hadn't read it in the notes either and was about to reopen them when her patient spoke again.

'You won't find anything in there,' Denise said, her voice suddenly quavering. 'All I want is for you to give me something to make me sleep. Going on past experience, I suppose you'll try and talk me out of that.'

'Is your not sleeping a recent problem?' Kate asked.

126

'More or less. It's the early morning that's worst. I wake at four or five and can't get off again. Look, you won't give me anything, will you?' cried the young woman, jumping angrily to her feet. 'What's the use of trying to talk to someone like you?' Bursting into tears and pushing her hands over her face, she turned to the door, but this time Kate was there before her. This was one occasion when she refused to be walked out on!

'I would like to help you,' Kate said calmly, 'and I know we didn't get off to a very good start regarding Sean, but all I ask is that you give me the opportunity to try to help you. I'm sure, if we examine your sleeping problem together, we can work out a resolution.' She reached out and gently took hold of the shaking shoulders, guiding the woman back to the chair where, unprotestingly, she resumed her seat.

Kate returned to her own chair. Slipping fresh tissues from her dispenser, she handed them across the desk. Denise Markham sank back and Kate was shocked to see how desolate and unhappy she looked.

'If you can tell me a little of what has been worrying you . . .?' Kate persevered and slowly, painfully, Denise Markham began to relate her sad story. It transpired that not only had her husband Gareth embarked on a long-standing affair, but he was the father of a two-year-old little girl. Unwilling to give up his mistress, he maintained a double life. Despite the pressure from Denise to make a choice, he stubbornly refused to break with either woman.

The situation had become so distressing that in spite of an attempt to keep Gareth's other family secret from her own family and friends the charade was now becoming intolerable, as were the financial and emotional pressures. Denise had lost her part-time job, a disaster, Kate realised, which had occurred because of the time she'd been forced to take off during the chickenpox episode and for which Denise obviously blamed her.

Eventually agreeing to prescribe a light, temporary sleeping medication, Kate suggested counselling, but at this Denise proudly shook her head. 'I don't want anyone to know,' she insisted. 'I didn't intend to tell you—I don't know why I let myself tell you.'

Kate realised she'd be unable to help if Denise didn't face the true facts of her dilemma, but she could sense that the young woman needed someone to confide in. 'Would you come to see me again?' Kate said. 'Or, if it's too difficult with the boys, I could make a house call.'

To her surprise Denise agreed. After accompanying her to the outer doors, Kate stopped at Reception and made a note in the book, thinking that at least she might be able to provide a minimum of support in what appeared to be her patient's increasingly isolated environment. It was by no means a substitute for counselling, but perhaps in time that option might become more appealing.

Rupert's next patient showed symptoms of acute ulcerative gingivitis, a painful gum disorder. This sixty-year-old smoker was prone to chest infections, but on this occasion his infected gums had produced ugly, crater-like ulcers. These had spread to his lips and the crevices of his cheeks, and an immediate visit to the dentist—which he had assiduously avoided for the last decade—was called for.

Although Kate suggested the temporary measure of a mouthwash containing hydrogen peroxide to ease the pain, there was no real solution other than the stringent removal of the plaque and calculus. Unable to provide any other alternative, Kate finally persuaded him to make an appoint-ment with his dentist.

In between patients Kate wondered how Toby was faring and resolved that her defence of him today would have to be the last time she ventured her opinion to Ben. It was almost four when her last booked patient walked in.

This young man had just taken a tumble from his bicycle and had sprained, but not fractured, his wrist. Kate prescribed a cold compress with ice and the support of a crêpe bandage. Accompanying him back out to Reception, she saw him on his way. She was beginning to think she'd weathered the worst of the day's problems when she saw Peter Frost limping towards her, accompanied by his bewildered-looking aunt.

'He's had his scan and blood tests,' she said with a sigh as Kate took them to her room. 'Then he came home from school today with these cuts. He accidentally fell over on the tarmac and I think they might need stitching. To be honest, I'll be relieved when those tests prove he has ME. He's as lifeless as a kitten.'

Kate bent to inspect the grazed knees and then remarking that she doubted if sutures were necessary, led Peter to one of the minor ops rooms. When he'd settled himself on the couch Kate set up a sterile area over his knees and began to remove the offending particles of asphalt with surgical tweezers. As Peter jumped nervously, several coins dropped to the floor from his pocket.

'Leave it for the moment,' Kate murmured, as she concentrated on her delicate task. 'Don't worry, no one's going to steal it.'

Almost at once Peter burst into tears. Astonished, Kate stopped what she was doing.

'What's the matter, Peter?' she asked in concern. 'Is what I'm doing too painful for you?'

The boy nodded, wiping his hand across his eyes. Although Kate could hardly believe her actions were causing him discomfort, she promised she'd try not to hurt him again.

130

Being doubly careful as she cleansed the grazes with antiseptic, she finally applied sterile dressings and told Peter he could climb down. Peeling off her gloves, she bent to retrieve the coins for him.

Kate was inclined to think her young patient's outburst was due to the ME rather than his grazed knees, and remembered the ease with which tears had sprung to her own eyes during her years as a sufferer. She regretted that she could do no more for Peter until she received his test results.

She advised his aunt once again to keep him away from school, and then completed her own surgery, finally signing prescriptions and taking them to Reception where she handed them over to Lesley.

'Dr Buchan came back in at four and did his surgery like a whirlwind,' Lesley remarked, as she arranged the prescriptions in alphabetical order for collection. 'He didn't mention Toby. I wonder what all the fuss was about?'

Kate shrugged, having no idea herself. She glanced around the waiting area and asked, 'Is there anyone else for me to see?'

Lesley raised her eyebrows, smiling. 'You're a glutton for punishment! Haven't you had enough for one day?'

Kate grinned. 'I'm hoping you'll say no, of course.'

'Only this, from Angie.' With a wry smile, Lesley handed Kate a handwritten message from Angie, suggesting they meet at seven at the sports centre for a swim. Kate's heart plummeted. Angie's idea of a swim was a toe-dip followed by an in-depth gossip over coffee. That could last the whole evening, especially if Angie was in full possession of the latest news—which, Kate reflected, dryly, she probably was.

When she returned home to collect her swimming gear the Mercedes was parked in the drive, and although there were lights on in the house there was no sign of life.

On Saturday morning she saw Tom taking Caesar for his stroll. On Sunday she caught a glimpse of Ben hurrying from the house to the Mercedes, obviously on call, but it upset her badly to think that he was avoiding her.

Monday brought news about Tessa, who was in Intensive Care. Her condition had stabilised and the leg wound and concussion had been dealt with, but there were still internal complications which were slowing her recovery. Rupert gave them updates, but no one liked to press him and Kate formed the impression he was relieved not to be asked.

Ben greeted her with a few words of conversation before surgery, but for the rest of the week he seemed to be avoiding her again and she guessed he didn't want to talk to her about Toby.

She was on call several evenings that week and she wasn't home until late, way past the boys' bedtime, so the opportunity to see Toby didn't arise. She became increasingly dismayed that his visits to her seemed to have stopped.

*　　　*　　　*

It was Saturday morning, as Kate was leaving the flat, when she next saw Ben. He was walking Caesar and she smiled apprehensively as he tugged the dog towards the house. He looked tired and drawn, she thought, his black hair rumpled across his head. Kate's heart sank as he seemed to avert his attention, arriving at the porch to let Caesar off the lead.

Kate unlocked the Volkswagen and slid in, feeling on the verge of tears at the deliberate snub. For a few moments she sat immobile, hurt and upset. He *had* thought she was interfering. He *had* resented her defence of Toby. No doubt he was justified as a father. Toby wasn't her son. She hadn't even known the family before May!

Her hand was on the ignition key when a shadow fell across her. She looked up, startled, and swallowed as she saw Ben's face.

'Good morning,' he said quietly, when she'd wound down the window.

'Hello.' Kate blinked, her cheeks flushing. Then she asked what she'd resolved not to ask. 'How are the boys?'

He made an effort to smile. 'Oh, fair, I suppose. I . . . er . . . I've been meaning to come across to The Den.'

She waited, holding her breath.

'I'm afraid that school business . . . well, it was more serious than we thought.'

Kate's heart dropped. 'In what way?'

He shrugged. 'Look, I don't want to detain you—you're obviously in a rush to get to surgery. Are you at home this afternoon?'

Kate nodded. 'Yes . . . I think so. Come over, if you like.'

He smiled. 'I'd like that.'

She watched him walk away, his broad shoulders swinging, a hand coming back to thrust the thick dark hair from his face as he entered the porch. As Kate drove to work she could make no sense of what was happening. Even if Toby had been in a fight, it certainly couldn't have been that bad. All boys got into fights. And for the headmaster to have suspended him—the whole notion seemed ridiculous.

*　　　*　　　*

When Kate arrived Hilly brought in her list, several of whom were temporary residents. There were sore throats and allergies and the usual collection of tummy upsets and heat-related complaints. At midday Kate replaced each of the temporary resident files back in their allotted section in the office, giving a sigh of relief that the morning was almost over.

134

However, back in her room the phone rang, and when Kate lifted it to her ear she heard a familiar voice which made her suspect that her thoughts of returning home were premature. 'It's Hugh,' explained Sara Conway tearfully. 'Since Wednesday I haven't been able to get him to talk to me. This morning he won't come out from his study. I don't think he has any pills in there, but I can't be sure.'

Kate glanced at her watch and wondered if Ben was at home. Should she phone him? It was something she'd prefer to avoid, especially if he was having trouble with Toby. As Sara was speaking, Kate felt torn. It would be easy enough to call at the cottage on her way home, but was Hugh Conway one patient whom she shouldn't attempt to visit on Ben's behalf?

Kate came to a swift decision and told Sara she'd ring her back. She was about to dial Ben's home number when Hilly appeared at the door.

'Mr and Mrs Sarkar are here,' she said. 'Mrs Sarkar isn't feeling very well. She isn't booked in, but do you think you could do the honours?'

Kate nodded. 'Just give me a moment, Hilly. I'll make this call and then I'll come out and talk to her.' Hilly nodded and disappeared. Kate dialled Ben's number, relieved that it wasn't too long before she heard the sound of his voice.

'I'll see Hugh right away,' he told her when

she'd finished explaining. 'You did right to phone me. Don't worry about phoning Sara back—I'll do it.'

Kate replaced the phone, feeling both guilty that she'd been forced to interrupt Ben's free time and relieved because she knew that a possible crisis might have occurred with Hugh.

Kate found Maneka sitting in the waiting area beside her husband. She wore a beautiful turquoise sari, and as she leaned back against the padded bench her hands went up to fold protectively over her stomach. 'Hello, Dr Ross. I wanted to choose some clothes for the baby and thought a short journey would be safe enough. I've felt so well lately. But suddenly in the shop I was dizzy and sick and just felt terrible.'

Her husband nodded, his face drawn as he helped her to her feet. 'For once the lift is working in the flats and I thought the change of scenery would be good for her. And so we made the journey—it's all my fault.'

'I'm sure no harm has been done,' Kate said reassuringly, 'and you were sensible to come here. It's probably nothing, but better to be safe than sorry.'

In her room Kate took Maneka to the couch and assisted her onto it. After taking her BP, she rearranged the folds of beautiful material and listened for the baby's heartbeat. A careful physical examination revealed nothing untoward. Maneka explained she had recently

136

had an ultrasound scan which had shown no abnormalities, and the results of blood tests and urinalysis had ruled out anaemia.

'I am hoping to have my baby in the birthing pool,' Maneka told Kate with a worried expression. 'There's nothing to say that I can't, is there?'

'You've discussed it with Dr Buchan?' Kate asked, and Maneka nodded. 'Then I can't see any reason why not,' Kate said with a shrug. Attempting once again to reassure her patient, Kate suggested a swift return home and the remainder of the day taken in rest.

After the Sarkars had left, Kate completed her correspondence, chatted briefly with Hilly and then left for home, wondering if Ben was still on his house call to the Conways.

The Mercedes was absent when she arrived, but propped against the wall of the workshop were two mountain bikes. As she turned the corner she saw two figures crouched on her doorstep. Tom sat with his elbows tucked across his knees and next to him sat Lisa, smiling apprehensively, her long, chestnut hair drawn up into a ponytail.

'Hello!' said Kate. 'This is a nice surprise.'

'Hello, Dr Ross,' they both said at once, and in the following silence Lisa looked at Tom who, even though he knew he was expected to speak, said nothing.

Guessing there must be some reason for this visit, Kate smiled. 'Well, I think cold drinks are

137

called for in this hot weather, don't you?'

It was a suggestion that was met by eager responses, and ten minutes later Kate was dispensing tall glasses of iced drinks in the flat.

It was Lisa who finally got around to explaining why they'd come. 'We don't think everyone's being very fair to Toby,' she said, as she sat next to Tom on the sofa, sipping her drink. 'He was only standing up for a friend—he wasn't the cause of the fight. This other person—well, he's just too scared to own up.'

Kate frowned. 'But why doesn't Toby explain this to your father, Tom?'

'He can't,' answered Tom defensively. 'Not really . . . because . . . well, Dad will say that he'll have to tell everything to the head, and he won't believe him because of—'

Lisa nudged Tom in the ribs and he went pink.

'You know, it really is for Toby to speak up and make a good case for himself. I'm sure if it's the truth the headmaster will listen,' Kate said gently.

'Some hopes,' Tom muttered. 'Anyway, we thought you might know what to do.'

Kate sighed. 'I'm not quite sure how I can help if Toby's sworn himself—and everyone else—to secrecy. But,' she added as she looked at two disappointed faces, 'leave it with me and I'll give it some thought.'

As she walked with Lisa and Tom into the hot afternoon sunshine, she gazed across at

138

the house. Another intrusion into Ben's private life would only cause him to resent her more, and she really had nothing to go on other than the faith of Tom and Lisa in Toby. But who would speak up for Toby if she didn't?

Her opportunity came sooner than she'd expected.

Dressed in cool white shorts and sneakers, she decided to sit in the sunshine at the rear of the flat. Taking a broad-brimmed sunhat, she slid into a deckchair and allowed herself to doze in the balmy heat. It was some time later when she awoke.

The sun had mellowed and the long shadows of the trees danced on the grass. She lay still for a few moments, soaking in the sounds of the birds, then felt her heart leap as a tall figure appeared beside her.

'Am I disturbing you?' Ben looked down at her. 'I thought for a moment you were sleeping.' He was dressed in Bermudas and a navy T-shirt, his silvery gaze studying her.

She smiled as she struggled to sit up. 'I must have dozed. It's so beautiful out here.'

He sank on the grass, stretching out long, bronzed legs and resting the palms of his hands on the grass. Kate drew her concentration together, her eyes sweeping over the firm lines of his strong, masculine body and the slightly open V of his T-shirt where tiny black hairs escaped and curled into the dark well of his throat.

'No problems, I take it, at surgery?' he asked with a frown.

'Only Maneka Sarkar. A shopping trip into Milchester was more tiring than she expected and I think she was concerned about not being fit enough to deliver in the birthing pool.'

'If the pregnancy goes according to plan and the pool is free at the time, I don't foresee any problems. Besides which, the stress factor is reduced in a case like this—where the patient has set her heart on a certain form of delivery—if both GP and obstetrician agree.'

Kate nodded. 'How was Hugh?'

He leaned forward to rest his brown elbows on his knees. He sighed. 'He'd locked himself in his study and I had to shoulder open the door. We found him sitting there, staring into space. This time he seems to have completely cut himself off from reality.' He pushed his hand into his hair and then looked up at her. 'I'd no choice but to admit him—something's triggered this depression, though I'm damned if I know what.'

They sat for a while in silence. Kate cast her mind back to the Friday of the accident and recalled how she'd glanced back as they'd driven off and had glimpsed Hugh standing in the garden, his face ashen as he'd stared towards the motorway.

She was about to mention it when she suddenly remembered her earlier conversation with the youngsters, and Hugh Conway receded from her mind. 'I was surprised to find Tom and Lisa waiting for me when I arrived home,' she said, and glanced at him cautiously.

'That sounds ominous.'

'They wanted to speak up for Toby,' she said, taking a deep breath, 'and asked for my help, although I couldn't get anything out of them about the fight at school.'

'Did they tell you he stands accused of stealing some money from the same boy he apparently punched?' Ben asked, one eyebrow raised.

Kate's face was incredulous. 'But Toby wouldn't steal,' she protested. 'That's absurd.'

Ben sighed. 'I'm afraid there's evidence to say he has. It was just a handful of loose change but, as his headmaster points out, the amount is irrelevant. Whether it was five pounds or fifty pence, it was still stolen from one of the prefects. Which means . . .' he added hesitantly, 'that we're in a worrying situation as the term ends. I've no idea if the police will be called in or even if the boy's parents will make an official complaint. I had planned to take the boys to Christchurch, as you know, but now, well, I'm not so sure.'

Kate sank back in her chair, her mind trying to bring to light something she couldn't quite capture, but as swiftly as it had come so it was gone. She frowned and, knowing it was

141

probably the last thing Ben wanted to hear, said, 'I don't believe Toby has taken anything that doesn't belong to him, and if he was in a fight with a prefect I just hope he was able to stand up for himself. And if anyone . . .' She stopped, her cheeks flushed as she ran out of breath, her hands clenched together in her lap as she thought of the injustice that Toby was suffering. About to continue, she glanced sharply at Ben who—to her astonishment—was laughing.

CHAPTER SEVEN

'I'm sorry,' Ben said, trying to control his amusement. His face looked so changed, his beautiful grey eyes looking almost luminous, Kate thought. He leaned forward and reached for her hand. 'You've such faith in Toby, haven't you?'

At his touch her breath stopped in her throat. 'Haven't you?'

His fingers tightened over hers. 'You know, in the week he's been grounded his main complaint has been that he hasn't been able to call here and talk to you. Not being allowed to go to the sports club or go out with his brother and Lisa doesn't seem to have worried him half as much as not coming here.'

Kate smiled. 'Yes, I've missed our games of

chess.'

'Does it surprise you to know we've a board at home and it's hardly ever used?'

She found herself staring into his eyes as his gaze fastened on hers. She held her breath, his fingers closing tightly around hers as they seemed, for a moment, to convey a wealth of unspoken feeling. She couldn't have said how long the moment lasted, only that it felt as if the seconds flew by and they appeared to be in a world of their own. A sensation was running down her spine that made her legs feel weak and shaky.

Voices in the garden beyond shattered the silence and Ben withdrew his hand, his eyes looking over her shoulder. The skin where his fingers had gripped her was warm and tingling, and she made a conscious effort not to reach out and slide her fingers over the sensitive area.

She felt, as he looked back at her, that something had changed between them, though she couldn't say exactly what. The attraction she felt towards him was part of it, but now there was more—something intangible, more difficult to identify. As these thoughts passed vaguely through her mind, Toby, Tom and Lisa came running around the corner, flushed with excitement.

'Mrs Howard says she's got scones and cream for tea,' shouted Toby breathlessly. 'And she asked if Dr Ross could bring some

143

lemonade because we've run out.'

Ben grinned at Kate. 'So much for your peaceful afternoon in the garden.'

It was then that Kate realised belatedly that she'd been included in the invitation, but before she could respond the youngsters were waiting at her open door.

'There's a bottle of lemonade in the fridge,' she called. 'Go up and help yourselves.'

They immediately disappeared through the open door and thundered up the stairs. Kate looked across at Ben and they both laughed. She rose to walk beside him across the lawns towards the house.

*   *   *

During the following week Kate received the results of Peter Frost's tests. She telephoned Mrs Mowbray, who brought a pale-faced Peter into surgery on Friday.

'As I've explained, there's no one specific test for ME,' Kate remarked to Peter's aunt, 'but the haematology results suggest abnormal lymphocytes. That indicates anaemia, which we can treat with iron. Also, Peter's positive tests of early antigen, or substances the body regards as foreign—which leads to a reactivated infection—have probably aided this current infection of his.'

'What about the scan?' asked Mrs Mowbray, frowning. 'Did that show up

144

anything?'

Kate nodded. 'The SPET scan indicates some abnormality in the brain stem, and, although research is still going on, we are inclined to believe this abnormality may be responsible for some of Peter's lower moods, certainly those in line with ME.'

'So, what happens now?' Mrs Mowbray asked. 'What do we do? He's really washed out again.'

'Well, to begin with we must take seriously the importance of rest. ME is characterised by chronic fatigue, and the avoidance of sports at school is extremely important. And when he's feeling ill, like this, I'm afraid he'll have to remain at home and, if necessary, in bed,' Kate said as she glanced at Peter. 'As we're now at the end of term this problem is irrelevant until September, and you can rest without worrying about missing your lessons.' Peter made no response, and Kate went on, addressing her remarks to Mrs Mowbray.

'A fresh-food diet is important, too, with the use of nutritional supplements such as A, B complex, C and E, as well as zinc. Each person responds differently to both traditional and alternative treatments. For instance, Efamol Marine—a combination of oils and essential fatty acids—has been found to help, and is something we might look at for Peter.' Looking back at the boy, she smiled. 'Perhaps I should have a look at your knees, Peter, just

145

to check they've healed.'

As Peter lay on the examination couch, he asked after Toby. Kate was aware that yet again the boy was on the brink of tears. She suspected that the events surrounding his ME and the isolation from his school friends were beginning to overwhelm him. She swiftly concluded her examination, taking care not to over-elaborate on the details of Toby's suspension.

That evening, on her way home, she called at the small semi-detached house on the outskirts of town where Denise Markham lived. The row of buildings, a long terrace of Victorian houses much like those she'd viewed with Toby when she'd been searching for accommodation, were set in a quiet area opposite a recreation ground, and the noise of boys, playing football, drifted pleasantly over the houses.

Denise opened the door and, without smiling, showed Kate into a room that led off the hallway. 'The boys are playing football across the road,' she said abruptly. 'They'll be in for their supper in a moment so I shan't be able to talk for very long.'

Kate glanced around the neat, clean front room. Although she wasn't offered a chair, she took a seat on the modern leather couch while Denise herself remained standing. Kate noticed there wasn't a toy in sight and she guessed this room was reserved for visitors only.

'I'm sorry you've made a journey for nothing,' Denise said sharply. 'I'd rather we forget what was said before. I'm all right now. I'd just had a bad day.'

'How are you sleeping?' Kate asked, not surprised that Denise had once again erected a barrier between them.

'The pills are helping,' answered Denise vaguely. 'At least I can sleep through the night now.'

Kate nodded thoughtfully. 'And the problems we were discussing—is there any hope of a resolution?'

At this her patient turned away and appeared to look out of the window, presumably for the return of her children. 'As I said, everything's all right now,' she said after a while. 'I know Gareth will come back. It's just a matter of time.'

Kate waited, sadly aware that the young woman was still in denial of her husband's attachment to his other family. She knew if she were to persist with her questioning she'd probably alienate Denise further so she avoided the issue of Gareth. She paused for a moment. 'Have you had any luck in finding another job?' she finally asked.

Denise turned, apparently relieved the question wasn't of a personal nature, shrugged. 'Not yet. I've put my name down at the school for a lunch supervisor's job. I might get something for September. The school holidays are always difficult.'

'What was the job you had to give up?' Kate asked cautiously, reflecting that Denise probably held her responsible for losing it.

Denise shrugged. 'I was a dental receptionist.'

Kate noted the abrupt sniff that probably denoted she was still in Denise's black books, but nothing was said. Eventually Kate stood up to leave. 'If you need to see me or Dr Greaves before your month's supply of medication is finished, just tell the receptionist on duty that I've asked for you to be fitted in that day. You shouldn't have any trouble seeing either one of us fairly quickly.'

Kate felt she'd achieved very little as she left the house, but as she arrived at the gate Sean and Mark, dressed in their football gear, crossed the road and ran up to her, bouncing the ball between them.

'Hello, Dr Ross,' Sean greeted her breathlessly. 'Have you seen Mum yet?'

Kate nodded. 'We've just had a chat. What team do you support?'

'Arsenal—they're wicked,' said Mark. Sean agreed, but his eyes were wary as they glanced back at the house.

'Is Mum all right?' he asked anxiously.

'Yes,' Kate reassured him, 'but I think she has your supper ready so I shouldn't keep her waiting.' At this, Mark shot off to the house, but Sean lingered, biting on his lip, obviously troubled.

'Our dad's taking us over to meet our baby sister tomorrow,' he said hesitantly. 'Is that what's making Mum upset?'

Kate shook her head. 'No, she didn't mention that to me, Sean. In fact, she said she was feeling much better.'

'Oh,' he said. He looked up at her and shrugged. 'I'd better go in, then.'

Kate watched him run in and wished she didn't feel so helpless. But if Denise Markham wouldn't accept help or even admit to a problem, there was nothing to be done. The boy had probably touched on the nub of the trouble, but if Denise was reluctant to discuss the situation then Kate knew she must accept she could do no more.

As she closed the gate slowly behind her she heard the boys shout out, and she turned to wave goodbye. She couldn't help thinking that whatever sort of man Gareth Markham was he was either selfishly insensitive or deliberately blind to the deep unhappiness he was causing his family.

*　　　*　　　*

It was a Saturday morning when Kate next saw Toby and Tom. They were on their bikes. Later in the day Toby, Tom and Lisa called at the flat, before being collected by minibus for

149

a trip to the local sports club. They brought her several punnets of strawberries, explaining they'd picked them during the afternoon at Lisa's father's farm.

'They look delicious,' Kate said gratefully. 'Would you like to eat some now?' But the minibus arrived at that moment and the driver gave a blast on the horn. Tom and Lisa sped off down the stairs.

Toby hesitated, his grey eyes coming up slowly to meet hers. 'I'm not grounded any more. Dad said one week was enough.'

Kate was relieved. 'Well, in that case, perhaps we can have a game of chess.'

'Yeah, great. And Grandma rang Dad and said she'd be really disappointed if we didn't visit them this summer so I think we'll be going after all.'

Good for Toby's grandmother, thought Kate as the minibus hooted again. Giving her another grin, Toby shouted goodbye as he bolted down the stairs.

It was some time later when Kate was about to slice the strawberries, intending to eat some of them for lunch, that she realised how much she would miss the presence of the twins about the house and gardens. They were becoming a part of her everyday life. She sighed and popped one of the succulent strawberries in her mouth, telling herself she'd better not become too attached. There was life after Milchester, and she'd better remember that!

*　　*　　*

Kate spent Sunday at the Lawrences', accepting Angie's offer of a roast and a stroll along the towpath in the afternoon. She wanted to get away from the house for a bit and try to clarify her thoughts. On one hand she felt she was becoming too involved in the Buchans' lives, and on the other she felt she couldn't help herself. After all, she saw a lot of the boys, and their father . . . well, he seemed to take up most of her thinking time.

She wondered if she should try to talk to Angie about it, but Angie would probably give her a sensible warning, tell her she still hadn't got over Julian and, worst of all, remind her about Mary Graham.

In the event, Miriam took her fishing net and the boys their rods and they sat in the glade of the trees by a stream so there was no time to speak on a more personal note.

By the time Kate got home it was half past five. She pulled up next to the Mercedes and saw Ben walking across the lawn. Whatever her thoughts during the day, she forgot every resolve at the sight of him. She panicked, of course, as she watched him come towards her.

'Hello. Where have you been all day?' He smiled, leaning his hip against the car as she got out.

'I lunched with Angie, then we went fishing

with the children.' She grinned. 'At least in theory.'

'So you haven't brought me home something tasty for supper?' His tone was wry.

'I'd love to say I have, but the most we caught were tiddlers.' She looked up at him. 'But I can offer you and the boys a drink . . .'

He shrugged. His lean, muscular body under his green T-shirt moved with the soft cloth. 'You've just missed the boys. They've gone to spend the night with a friend—I finally gave in after Toby's grounding. And I thought they could probably do with a change of scenery. But if the offer still stands . . .'

She smiled and nodded. 'I think I've a cold lager in the fridge.'

'Sounds wonderful.' He held out his hand and she slipped hers into it. 'I've missed you.'

She held her breath. 'Have you?'

'I'm glad you came home.'

The evening was as soft as silk around them as they walked slowly together across the lawn, his hand sliding around her waist, their bodies brushing gently. Birds were singing and a soft summer's breeze teased their skins. Kate thought what a perfect evening it was and that she must be dreaming. It felt so right to be here—so good—in this little area of garden that she was beginning to feel was almost hers. Right or wrong, that was the way it felt.

The door closed behind them and she led the way upstairs, her heart beginning to run into overdrive as she felt him behind her. She knew she'd have to turn around and look into his eyes and see everything there that she didn't want to see—and yet that she did.

'I'll just get us a drink,' she said, without looking at him, but he gripped her hand and pulled her back towards him. In her small sitting room they seemed to be entirely in a world of their own—an unreal, make-believe world, hundreds of miles away from reality.

'Don't go,' he whispered. She felt his hands slide around her neck and remove the band that had kept her hair tidily in place at her nape. 'Oh, Kate, you look lovely tonight.'

She knew what was going to happen next. And she knew she was going to let it happen. And he knew . . .

'I don't want a drink,' he said quietly, lifting her chin between his palms. 'I want you. My feelings haven't altered since that first time . . . after Glyn's party.' His voice was gruff, but his face was so close she could see the lines of need engraved on it, changing its shape and expression—a reflection of her own need and desire, she thought as she lifted her fingers to run over his grainy, warm skin.

'Not here . . .' she said softly. Seconds later she stood before him in the bedroom, her body trembling as he began to undo the small pearl buttons of her blouse. What would she look like as he took off her clothes? Would she disappoint him? It had been so long since

153

Julian. Could she remember what it was like to make love properly, to lie alongside a man and be touched . . . held, caressed?

Julian hadn't wanted to touch or hold her when she'd been ill. For a while they'd even slept in separate bed-rooms. She'd wound up feeling unattractive and unfeminine.

Now Ben was staring at her as she stood before him, his eyes burning with desire, their pupils expanding to a deep, lustrous black, his breathing shallow and his skin so hot she could feel its warmth without touching him.

'You're beautiful, Kate,' he told her as her bra slipped away. 'You're so beautiful, but I want you to want this too . . .'

She shuddered. She wanted him so much and that was the trouble. She wanted him with desperation, a confused emotion that she'd never felt in her life before.

She took off her skirt, unbuttoning it from the side and letting it fall to the ground. She saw his eyes glide down over her hips and thighs and legs. Her response was predictable, an immediate rush of anxiety about how she must look, how unattractive she must be—a legacy from Julian which seemed to have been stamped on her soul. She felt like squirming away, but the expression in Ben's eyes as they came up to meet hers was hungrier than ever.

'Oh, God, Kate . . .' He lifted her in his arms, took her to the bed and laid her down. She heard his intake of breath as she lay there, and she reached out to touch him as he stripped off his T-shirt and jeans to reveal the pattern of tight brown muscles that rippled under his skin. He bent to caress her with soft, slow strokes of his tongue.

He crushed her against him, his powerful grip eliminating all doubts as she travelled into a world of her own. Her fingers discovered the secret nooks and crannies of his body, foraging in the tangle of dark chest hair that spread from shoulder to shoulder and down into a silky arrow of darkness at his abdomen.

With a forwardness she could hardly believe of herself, she was stripping off his shorts and he her panties, each revelling in the first, shattering, stunning awareness of their bodies and the intimacy of their love-making. Soft gasps came against her ear and she, too, was making similar noises, sounds indefinable and almost feral, the skill of speech almost forgotten in their search for fulfilment.

'Kate, I want you so much I'm afraid to go on,' she heard him whispering into her hair. She wanted him too, much, much more than she could believe it was possible to want someone.

'Oh, Ben . . . don't stop now.' Her whisper was ragged as he lifted her against him, his mouth dragging down over her neck to her breasts, sending a thousand ecstatic quivers through her bloodstream, his mouth running over their peaks with untamed, glorious wantonness that left her panting and breathless.

They seemed to move in rhythm, like the ebb and flow of the tide, each sensing, scenting, peaking and lifting on the waves of their need. His cry was passionate and primitive, hers softer but no less needy. Their final coupling, a shuddering of bodies and melting of emotions, flowed through skin and bone and muscle.

When each of them had subsided, breathless and damp with exertion, he hugged her to him, kissing her with small, slow, loving kisses that were more than words, more than any other action could convey.

After a while Kate realised they must have slept because she woke up suddenly as he moved sleepily beside her, his dark head indenting the pillow. She stared at him, drinking in the pleasure of watching him at her leisure but worried there was something to get up for, something she'd forgotten. Then she realised that the boys weren't there, neither of them were on call and for once time was their own.

He must have felt her gaze because he, too, awoke. Touching her lips with his fingers, he slid them across her cheeks and into her hair. They made love again, this time without desperation and with a slow, growing confidence that made their loving more real, more perfect. When it was over she lay curled

156

up with her back against his chest. Evening was falling outside, smooth shades of grey and pink sky showing beyond the trees.

'The boys won't be coming home?' she whispered.

'No. Not until tomorrow. Tom's being dropped at school. Toby here.'

'It's so unfair,' Kate breathed. 'He must feel dreadful.'

'That's why I let him go today.'

Kate was silent, then she turned and wrapped her arms around him. She looked into his eyes and wondered if he'd thought about children . . . more children. If he and Mary Graham had ever got to this point in their relationship . . .

'What are you thinking?' he asked her softly, teasing her nose with the tip of his finger. 'You're not regretting this?'

She shook her head. 'No, but we weren't very careful—were we?' She hesitated, lifting her brows. 'Or at least I wasn't.'

He closed his eyes and let out a sigh. 'Oh, God, Kate. I'm sorry. I just didn't think.' He brought her slowly to him in a hug. 'You're not on the Pill?' he asked.

'No. I didn't expect to find myself . . . here, with you.'

She wondered if he really was as sorry as he looked and how he'd react if their thoughtlessness produced the terrible complications in their lives that they had to

157

deal with in surgery every day, and which had only seemed to affect other people.

He said quietly, 'I can't believe I let us take such a risk.'

She wrapped her arms around him, laying her head on his chest. He stroked her hair and sighed. 'Look, I'll have to go across to the house and see to the dog.' She felt his withheld breath. 'Do you want me to come back tonight?'

She looked up slowly. 'Yes . . . if you want to come back.'

He held her very tight. 'Of course I do. And I'll . . . I'll make sure I'm prepared this time. Kate . . .'

'It's all right,' she whispered. 'Really.'

He got out of bed and tugged on his clothes silently. 'Back soon,' he called across the room, before closing the door behind him. 'I'll leave the door on the latch behind me.'

Alone in the flat, Kate turned restlessly in the bed. To even consider having a child at this stage was the height of irresponsibility, and Ben was obviously angry with himself for exposing them to such a risk. But as she lay there, staring at the ceiling, the thought of a baby trickled through her like warm, melting honey. Guiltily she tried not to think of the feel of a small, wrapped bundle in her arms, pressed against her breast.

What was happening to her, for goodness' sake? She was realistic enough to know that at her age all her hormones were clamouring towards child-rearing, but at this point in her life . . . no, it would be madness. The bitter disappointment she'd experienced with Julian's negative attitude towards babies had been blunted by the ME, but now the thought of a child of her own seemed to echo painfully the physical longing that she had smothered inside her.

After what seemed an eternity later he returned. He joined her in the shower and they made love again. The night stretched gloriously ahead of them, with supper on their knees on the sofa, talking late into the night and hours of loving—this time accompanied by caution.

*   *   *

They set the alarm for six so that Ben could arrive back at the house before Toby was dropped off before school. It was a close call as they showered and lingered over breakfast together, only realising when Ben left that it was almost eight.

He looked in to see her mid-morning, poking his head around the door between patients. It felt a clumsy moment. Lesley arrived with an emergency house visit for Ben and they both tried to act normally—without a great deal of success. Her cheeks glowing, Kate buried her head in her paperwork under

Lesley's astute gaze.

She was home late that evening, and it wasn't until the next day that he walked into the office where she was studying the post, took her in his arms and kissed her recklessly. She pushed him away as footsteps passed by the office door.

She found herself laughing softly as she claimed back her chair. 'Someone's bound to walk in,' she said in a flustered voice as she stared up at him.

'So . . . when can I see you next? Tell me and I'll leave you alone.' He ignored her protest and came to perch on the desk, tugging a strategically placed pin from her hair, which fell heavily around her shoulders, flying around her face. But she couldn't be angry with him. He looked so wonderful, dressed in a green and white striped shirt and a bottle-green tie, the long lines of his legs covered elegantly in dark trousers. His hair was combed back in a thick, smooth wave from his forehead. A now-familiar aroma pervaded the room—tangy and with a hint of lemon, it filled her nostrils and she took a breath, raising her eyes to his.

'We'll talk later,' she promised, 'when I can concentrate.'

His eyes moved over her hungrily, lingering on the feminine pale pink suit she wore, its slender curves moulding her body softly and outlining its delicacy. 'What have you got there?' he asked eventually, when he was unable to make her blush any more than she already was.

She looked down at the paper she was clutching. 'It's Sheila Dobson's report, the lady I diagnosed as having acromegaly.'

He frowned, leaning forward. 'Bad news?'

She nodded. 'The scan's confirmed a tumour.' She sighed, and passed him the results to read. 'I'll be referring her to a surgeon.'

Dark eyebrows lifted in concern as the grey eyes moved quickly over the report. Then he looked up. 'And Sara Conway? When is her laparoscopy scheduled for?'

'Next week, I believe.'

He seemed to be pondering this for a while and then, almost making her jump again, he leaned down and brushed his mouth over her lips. His eyes twinkled with amusement as he whispered he was about to start surgery and wouldn't pester her further. She smiled as he stood up, but she was totally unprepared for his next remark.

'I've decided to take the boys to Christchurch after all,' he told her, as he sank his hands into his trouser pockets. 'Disappointing their grandparents is something I want to avoid and, besides, we can't be expected to put our lives on hold for the whole of the summer. So . . . I thought I'd set off on Friday around lunchtime and spend a long, indulgently lazy weekend at the seaside.'

Kate managed to smile. 'Oh, that will be wonderful for you all.' His eyes rested questioningly on her face and she felt a dart of disappointment inside her, almost a physical ache, as she stared into the silvery grey pools. 'And the forecast's good,' she added brightly. 'No rain.'

He looked at her blandly. 'No. No rain.'

'What about Caesar? Do you want me to look after him for you?'

'No.' He shrugged. 'We've found quite reliable kennels . . . and, anyway, you'll be too busy.' A broad grin spread across his face. 'We were hoping you'd join us,' he said with a chuckle. 'That is, if you fancy staying at an enormous old house on the cliffs, with lots of draughts and creaky old corridors. The views are good, though—right over the Solent. Superb on a sunny day. I think you'd enjoy it.'

Kate stared at him. 'But your parents don't know I even exist!'

He looked under his dark lashes. 'Oh, they know you exist all right. They've had a weekly telephone commentary on your existence ever since you moved into The Den.'

'But I can't remember if I'm on call or in surgery—'

'Let's cross that bridge when we come to it,' he broke in. 'However, if you've other plans . . .'

'Oh, no, not at all.' She grinned. 'It's just such a surprise, that's all.'

'So it's settled?'

'Well . . . yes, I suppose it is,' she said with a laugh.

'Good,' he said quietly. 'I'd better go and try to juggle the rotas, then.'

It wasn't as easy as he'd thought, they realised as Kate was on call and Meg, who would have substituted, had family of her own coming to stay. So it was finally arranged for the following week, which was even better in the long run because no one seemed to notice that she and Ben had a half-day at the same time.

*   *   *

At two o'clock on Friday of the following week, she arrived back at the house to find Ben stowing cases into the Mercedes's boot, having changed into light-coloured linen trousers and a creamy, short-sleeved shirt with an open neck. 'Hello, there,' he called. He came around to open her door, bending down as if to kiss her.

'Where are the boys?' She looked anxiously at the house.

'Probably spying on us as we speak,' he said warningly, and kissed her all the same.

As she scrambled out past him she mumbled something about luggage, and he laughed. 'I'll come with you. Can't have you hauling cases across the lawn.'

She giggled as they strolled together. 'You're an incorrigible tease.'

'Absolutely—where you're concerned.' He gave her a lascivious grin, sliding his hand around her waist. 'Don't worry, Tom's on the phone to his lady love and Toby's checking with Mrs Howard. She's terrified we're not going to leave her with a fully operational security system.' He laughed. 'She's still nervous of upsetting the security codes when she leaves tomorrow for Oxford. Once the whole lot went off and ever since she's gone in terror of it.'

They were still laughing when they arrived at Kate's door. After she'd opened it he pulled her into his arms and kissed her properly.

'Someone really is going to catch us one day,' she sighed.

'I'll risk it,' he whispered as he let her go. 'Don't rush. I'm taking the dog to the kennels first.'

She nodded. 'I've just a few more things to get ready.'

'Make certain you include beachwear,' he told her with a smile as he headed off. 'The boys insist on showing you their favourite cove.'

As Kate showered and changed into a pair of white summer trousers and a deep blue tie-waist top, she felt almost too excited to think

164

about eating. She hadn't quite been able to believe it was really happening, though over the last week it had been impossible to differentiate between her own excitement and the twins'.

Having eaten one sandwich, she tried to think what it was she'd forgotten. She only remembered on her way out—a bottle of good wine and some Belgian chocolates she'd bought for Ben's parents. She'd worried whether they really had asked her to stay or whether it had all been Ben's idea and his parents would have to cater for her at the last moment.

Ben and the boys were already waiting when she got back. Toby and Tom sat in the back of the car, their peaked caps turned the wrong way on their heads. Kate laughed and joined in their teasing, aware of Ben's gaze as she slid into the passenger seat beside him.

She felt wonderful, she realised, putting all doubts to the back of her mind. She intended to concentrate on one thing only this weekend—enjoying herself. Glancing at the man beside her, so handsome and smiling with soft grey eyes that made her heart turn over every time she looked into them, she somehow knew she would.

CHAPTER EIGHT

Ben wiped the inside of the mask, shook the sand from the fins and laid the wetsuit on the back of the camping chair. 'This one should fit,' he said with a grin, sweeping his eyes over Kate's slender, slowly tanning body. 'It's lucky that we've kept so many spares—the boys grow so quickly they grow out of them every few years, but that one should fit you snugly.'

The sun was afternoon-hazy now and it felt good on her skin, not too penetrating. That, she thought, couldn't be said for Ben's gaze as he drank her in, the grey eyes telling her how good she looked in her new blue swimsuit, cut high over her long legs. Her skin had mellowed to a golden softness. Her blonde hair, already lightened by the sun, had streaks the colour of rich honey running through it.

Abandoned by the boys as they'd charged off to the water, Kate was left with Ben for her first lesson in snorkelling. He stood beside her, tall and dark, his skin bronze. Even before they'd come away, Kate had noticed that his physique had been enhanced by a healthy-looking tan, and now the long brown hands that held the mask were a beautiful chestnut as they slipped over the glass.

Kate had watched him running in and out of the water with the boys, his tall, agile body slippery from sea water. From early on today they'd been on the beach, enjoying the bubbling surf that came tumbling over the smooth sand of the secluded cove near Christchurch.

Laura Buchan had packed them a picnic and had made sure Kate had been provided with barrier cream. Kate liked Ben's parents. They'd made her feel instantly at home in their lovely cliffside home, which hadn't in the least matched Ben's unflattering description of a draughty old house. The boys had been placed, as usual, in their large attic room, and to Ben's amusement they'd given her a bedroom next to his on the second floor, his eyes briefly catching hers with a mischievous glint as he showed her the way to it.

This morning, Saturday, she'd woken to hazy sunlight streaming in the window and the smell of salt in the air. They had breakfasted early, at seven, and had left the house, complete with picnic, ready for a dip before nine. The water had been freezing but wonderfully invigorating. Kate had swum out to sea until she was breathless and then they'd played ball in the shallow water until they'd finally exhausted themselves.

They'd lain on the beach under the brolly, and the boys had regaled her with stories of fish six feet long swimming off the cove. She'd only realised they'd been teasing when Ben had thrown back his head and laughed.

After lunch Torn and Toby had snorkelled again. They'd pulled Kate into the water and demonstrated the technique, their brown bodies slipping like eels below the surface. Kate had used the mask and had dipped her head tentatively under the surface as they had shown her, but now it was left up to Ben to complete her instruction.

'You'll soon get the hang of it,' he told her as he helped her with the wetsuit, his fingers brushing her skin and causing a little current of electricity to run erratically under the fabric. She shivered. His hands smoothed over the wrinkles and he caught her gaze as he came around to take a look at the fit. Somehow the act of wriggling into the suit was very feminine, although she'd always thought how ungainly the suits looked—but that had been before she'd experienced how the suit cleaved perfectly to her curves.

He reached across to the zip, grinning. 'Now, this is a temptation,' he whispered as she breathed in.

She giggled. 'Don't you dare.'

'What would you do if I did?' He wiggled the hook threateningly.

'Never speak to you again,' she assured him swiftly.

He grinned again and slid the zip into place. 'Comfy?'

'I . . . I think so. What about those things?' She pointed to the flippers.

'Not very elegant,' he agreed, 'but necessary. They'll be heavier than you think. Don't worry, I'll carry you down to the water's edge. It'll be easier.' He helped her put them on, then lifted her into his arms.

'Are you sure this is how people go snorkelling?' she said with a laugh, clinging to his shoulders.

'It depends on the teacher-pupil relationship,' he murmured lazily, a rueful glint in his eye. 'Hold tight.'

At the water's edge he lowered her and slipped his mask over his head, having drawn his finger over his tongue and wiped the glass. 'Keeps the glass from fogging up,' he told her, and Kate did the same.

'Aren't you going to wear a suit, too?' she asked as they waded in.

'I would if we went further out, but we'll just swim locally where it's calm and warm. You'll see fish and seaweed and plenty of things you didn't think were there when you were swimming.' He showed her how to use the snorkel air-hose, biting down on the mouthpiece. 'Clear the hose by blowing hard if the water creeps inside. And remember to kick your legs without bending your knees.' He grinned. 'I'll be beside you all the time. Promise.'

That was what she was worried about, she realised. It was difficult enough to concentrate on dry land with him beside her, let alone in the clear, warm, blue water, and her heart was hammering as he squeezed her hand and they floated on its frothy surface. But once she was under and her breathing relaxed she forgot where she was.

Ben had been right. It was another world down there. Tiny, silvery fish skimmed past her mask. The colours were luminous—satin-green rocks glimmered from bright yellow sand. Flatfish and crabs scuttled into holes. No wonder the boys loved this cove, she thought, entranced.

Once or twice seaweed engulfed her, but then she felt Ben's arm around her waist, his strong body matching her speed as she kicked along with her feet, remembering to keep her legs straight. At one point he clamped his thumb and one finger together in a circle to indicate she was doing fine, and she felt ridiculously pleased with herself.

After a while she began to wonder why she'd never tried to snorkel before. Just as she'd dipped again for her third attempt, she almost jumped out of her skin. Tom and Toby came streaking up to her, making ghostly grimaces through their masks. Her own mask filled with water and before she knew it she was panicking, trying to breathe in a fog of bubbles. A strong pair of arms wrapped themselves around her, pulling her upwards to break the surface.

Treading water, she gasped for air, her

lungs sore with the exertion. 'I thought I was drowning!' she gulped.

'Scram, you two!' Ben growled at the boys. Still laughing, they splashed off, but Kate managed to see the funny side of it.

'I think I've just drunk several gallons of sea water!' she admitted, blinking the salty water from her eyes.

'Don't let them put you off. We'll go down again when you've got your breath back,' he told her, grinning.

And so they did, this time swimming amongst a colony of silvery-green fish. 'The locals call it a moon fish, because of its colouring,' he told her when they surfaced. 'And it seems to glow. On a day like this when the water is clear, you can always see them here.'

Kate couldn't get enough of the place. They went down again and again. Ben swam beside her, his body rubbing against her wetsuit as the current swirled and ebbed around them. Finally, laughing and breathless, he dragged her from the sea. They fell on the sand and she lay back panting. 'I love it,' she gurgled. 'I could stay here all day.'

'We have,' he told her, lying next to her on his side. He held his hand out and she threaded her fingers through it, then jerked it away.

He laughed. 'Don't worry, the boys are still in the water.'

She giggled, feeling like a teenager. 'I've had a wonderful time,' she admitted, her eyes meeting his.

'And it's not over yet.' He leaned forward on his elbow, reaching out to touch her long, wet hair. 'But you're right. It's been a perfect day.'

*   *   *

Dinner that evening with Laura and Edward was just as perfect. They ate alfresco on the balcony, overlooking the cliffs. Kate couldn't help thinking, as she looked at the expanse of glimmering ocean, how she'd felt earlier—how sensuous and smooth the sea water had been as she'd swum with Ben that afternoon.

The soft smile on her lips was mistaken, she hoped, for enjoyment of Laura's delicious chicken baked in a spicy wine sauce. The boys were on their best behaviour and didn't tease her too much. And Ben was relaxed and more at ease than Kate had ever seen him before.

Edward Buchan was an older version of his son. His dark hair was now an iron grey, his bronzed skin the evidence of an all-weather swimmer. A retired obstetrician, he was still, at seventy, a handsome man. Ben's mother, Laura, small-boned and elegant, obviously adored her grandsons, and it was her tactful suggestion that Ben take Kate into Christchurch to show her the harbour at night, leaving the boys with them.

172

So finally they found themselves alone as they strolled along the quay, watching the last boats moor for the night. Over a hundred feet above them the golden fish of the priory pointed westwards. 'The story goes,' Ben told her as his arm slipped around her waist, 'that the carpenter who worked on the priory disappeared mid-construction. A beam had fallen short of its length over the altar—he was devastated. Miraculously, the next day, it was extended to the right length, but the poor man was never heard of again.'

Kate shuddered and he turned her gently towards him, his hands running over her arms. Then he bent to kiss her, his fingers brushing back her hair. 'Snuggle into me,' he murmured, sliding her hands around his neck.

It was later, as they walked beside the river, that they talked about his brother, Miles. 'Kay and Miles live in Scotland,' he told her. 'Miles is in obstetrics, as Dad was. They've two teenagers, Emma and Sasha—a bit older than the twins.'

'Are you and Miles close?' Kate asked.

He nodded. 'Though we didn't see much of one another when I was married,' he admitted. 'Miles and Paula didn't get on.' He shrugged. 'Paula was working for the same charity organisation as me in South Africa. That's how we met. Miles came over once or twice, but it was clear they were chalk and cheese.' He said in a quieter voice, 'Paula loved that country.

She never wanted to leave. But when the boys were born I wanted security for them. And at the time, rightly or wrongly, I thought it was the best thing to come home.'

'I'm sure you only did what you thought was best,' Kate said, sensing the regret in his voice.

He shrugged again. 'Paula wasn't interested in general practice. She missed South Africa and the friends she'd made there.' His face darkened as they reached the car and he leaned against it, staring at the ground. 'If I hadn't insisted we move back to England, she might still be alive.'

'But it was an accident. No one can foresee an accident,' Kate protested.

He looked up at her. 'I was responsible for making a decision that deprived the boys of their mother.'

'That's absurd, Ben.' She shook her head. 'You're just tormenting yourself, carrying unnecessary guilt. None of us know what might happen tomorrow—just walking across the road is a risk.'

After a while he reached out and pulled her to him and she slid her arms around his waist. They stayed there together quietly, listening to the soft breeze skidding through the masts and the last gulls flapping over the water.

She shivered, her head on his chest. She could hear his breathing, feel his heart under her ear. She suddenly realised she knew why he hadn't married since Paula—the twins were

174

more than enough for him, the responsibility of another emotional tie just too much to bear. She couldn't blame him. She'd never been married to Julian, but the loss had been bad enough. Even now she felt vulnerable to her own confused emotions. And being with Ben wasn't helping. She knew there was no future here. That she was just dreaming. Yet she hadn't been able to stop herself . . .

'I'd better get you home,' he told her, running his lips across the top of her head. 'I don't want to, but I think we must.'

She nodded. 'Do you think they'll still be up?'

'My parents? No. They'll have gone to bed. The boys should have crashed out too.' He said in a low tone, 'Kate, I want to be with you tonight.'

She looked up at him. Paula was still as much a part of his life as any living human being. She knew why Mary Graham was poised on the edge of Ben's life. Because he kept her there.

Kate thought of Julian and made a fleeting comparison. They'd shared a home, friends and social scene. Had it not been for the ME, they'd intended to share a life together—not that she could now believe that life would have been happy. Illness had tested their relationship and it had failed. So how much deeper had Ben's own suffering been, with others depending on him for their happiness?

And how much firmer his resolve not to take responsibility for another person's happiness again?

Linking her hands with his, she managed to smile. 'Do you think that's a very good idea?'

He grinned. 'It's a big house. And we are next door to each other.' He drew her gently towards him. 'But you'd feel better if we didn't, wouldn't you?'

She nodded. 'Let's . . . let's wait, enjoy the rest of the weekend . . .'

He kissed her slowly, opening her mouth against the pressure of his lips, a kiss urgent and full of desire. 'All my good intentions have evaporated,' he whispered huskily. 'Rational thought seems to go out of the window when you're near me.' For a long while, it seemed, they stared at each other, and then their lips met in a fierce, abandoned embrace. Somewhere a gull cried out piercingly, a sweet-sad sound that Kate knew she would always associate with the feeling inside her at this moment. She'd never hear the cry of a gull again without thinking of this night.

*   *   *

Early on Sunday morning they visited the beach again. They managed to resume their light-heartedness in front of the boys, but Kate sensed that something had changed between them. She tried not to worry at the thought,

176

and concentrated on her snorkelling, diving independently of the men and discovering a small coin buried in the sand—a real Victorian penny.

At midday they went back to the house. The sun was at its highest and so everyone lazed in the cool. In the afternoon Laura and Edward took them to the old town for sightseeing. They wandered through the castle ruins and along Mill Stream to the Almoner's Wall, where two hundred years ago the poor received their dole of bread and ale or—if they weren't so fortunate—were interned in the workhouse.

By the museum she caught Ben's eye as he stood, his hands thrust deeply in his pockets, a little apart from the group. She would remember this moment, too, she thought, as she would their intimacy last night. His aroma came to her on the breeze, making her dizzy with longing, but soon Toby turned back to her, took her hand and drew her into the family circle, his fingers tugging her away.

That evening they ate as they had before, on the terrace. Laura made salad and home-made bread. They broke open the wine and chocolates, drank coffee and sat in the sun. Later Ben drove them back to the beach and they ambled along the shore, discovering shells and driftwood. The silver-grey sky was speckled with gold and pink and the waves tumbled up to their bare toes with a spent, lazy

177

energy.

The Buchans had warm drinks awaiting them on their return, and as her head touched the pillow that night Kate fell into a deep, dreamless sleep, exhausted by fresh air and exercise.

*   *   *

Kate rose early the next morning, at six. The boys were tired and didn't wake. Laura and Edward cooked breakfast, and waved them off.

They both had surgeries at eleven and Kate had to pick up her car from the house. Ben said he'd check with Mrs Howard and, if there was time, collect Caesar from the kennels. But as soon as he'd dropped her luggage at the top of the stairs, he dragged her into his arms and hugged her close. 'Oh, God, I've been waiting ages to do this.' He sighed. 'I never thought we'd be on our own.'

'I had a wonderful time,' she whispered.

A feeling of magic flowed through her body that made her quake with longing as she found herself driving to work, wondering if the last forty-eight hours had really happened. Her mood soon changed as the reality of the surgery engulfed her. The phone was ringing in her room as she entered, and by the time she'd answered it Lesley was standing at the door, asking if she wanted the post.

Signalling to Lesley to enter, she frowned into the receiver. 'What's the problem, Hilly?'

'Denise Markham,' Hilly answered, sounding harassed. 'She's in a terrible state. Will you talk to her or shall I ask her to come in—or what?'

Kate paused. 'Put her through, Hilly—and have we a vacant space?'

'I'll try to fit her in,' Hilly promised.

Kate glanced up, catching Lesley's eye. She realised that even if the Friday half-day she and Ben had taken off hadn't been noticed, their return at eleven this morning certainly had. Nodding her thanks for the post, she turned back to the telephone.

'Denise?' Kate sat down as Lesley disappeared. 'Where are you?'

'At . . . at home,' the muffled voice said.

'Have you anyone with you—the boys?'

'N-no. They're with their father and *her.*'

Kate was relieved the boys were safe, despite Denise's bitter tone. 'What's happened?' she probed gently.

Denise poured out her story. Gareth had finally made his choice and had left with the boys yesterday morning when Denise had been at the supermarket.

'When I came back,' Denise sobbed, 'there was just a note. Gareth said he'd gone for good and taken the boys with him. I just don't know what to do with myself.'

'I'm in surgery until one,' Kate told her

179

calmly. 'I'll call by then or, if you prefer, come in now to the surgery. Could you ring for a taxi?'

'N-no,' said Denise. 'I'll wait till you come.'

Managing to extract a promise that she would sit down with a cup of tea and turn on the television to keep her mind occupied, Kate rang off. A few minutes later Hilly rang to say that Gareth Markham was on Rupert's list, should she want to know.

Kate spoke to Rupert, who explained he was aware of Gareth's problems but not that he now had his sons living with him. He offered to contact him if necessary and try to sort out something. However, the best news of all was about Tessa, who was well enough to be discharged from hospital. Tessa's family had suggested that as soon as she was released from hospital they'd have her home to recuperate. Although Tessa lived and worked in the City, her parents lived in Banbury and Rupert was pleased that he'd be able to visit her more frequently.

Kate was about to begin her surgery when the phone rang again. 'Listen,' Ben told her hurriedly, 'I've swapped my on-call for tonight with Bal, which means I'm not on until Thursday. And Mrs Howard has just rung me to say she's been called away to her daughter's. The kids have got flu. That means we've got the house to ourselves tonight.'

'Great.' She hesitated. 'I'll cook, if you like.'

'I was hoping you'd suggest that.'

They laughed easily together, but when Kate put the phone down she sat looking at it for a few moments, afraid to think of how happy she was.

At one, she left for Denise Markham's.

She found the front door ajar and Denise sitting alone in the kitchen. In the garden beyond a bicycle and football lay idly on a patch of overgrown grass.

'He took them when my back was turned,' Denise said numbly. 'She must be laughing at me. She must think I'm a real fool. She had his baby—now she's taken my babies, too.'

Kate sat at the table, reaching out to touch Denise's cold hand. She looked pale and thin, and had dark, rough patches beneath her eyes.

'What's going on here?' said a voice from the doorway. A woman, who was carrying two full plastic bags, stood there, frowning at them. 'Who are you?' she demanded of Kate.

'This is my doctor,' said Denise, before Kate could respond.

'Is she ill?' asked the woman. 'I'm her mother, Mrs Horgan. I come to visit every Monday. Where are the boys?'

Kate glanced at Denise. 'I'll make a cup of tea,' she offered, 'and perhaps you can tell your mother what's happened.'

A few minutes later there were raised voices in the front room. Denise was shouting that she'd only married Gareth in order to get away from home and her parents' domination. In return, the older woman was reminding her daughter that Gareth Markham was an unsuitable husband, a man with no prospects and a roving eye.

Kate poured hot water into the teapot, then heard foot-steps running up the stairs. Denise's mother walked into the kitchen. 'So he's finally made up his mind,' she snapped.

'If you mean Gareth,' Kate agreed, 'yes, it appears so.'

'He's a charmer, that's the trouble.' Mrs Horgan took the mugs from the cupboard and put them on the table. 'My husband and I knew it from the moment we laid eyes on him, but she would never listen, of course. And it's the kids who suffer, more's the pity. Denise thinks I didn't know about my son-in-law and his fancy lady, but I saw them out together a couple of weeks back—with the little girl.'

Kate paused. 'Will you be able to stay with your daughter if I give her something to make her rest?'

She nodded. 'Mind you, it'll just show that other little madam what it's like, having to keep control of two young boys. I'll bet she'll have her eyes opened!'

Privately, Kate felt that Denise was in no fit state to cope with the boys at all at the moment, and a break from the children would be to her advantage. 'Is it possible for you to speak to Gareth on your daughter's behalf,' she ventured, 'and try to arrange a date when the boys might be coming back?'

'I'm not getting involved,' the older woman protested. 'I'll do what I can for Denise, but I'm not speaking to him. It's a disgrace what he's done and he should be made to pay for it.'

Kate administered a sedative to Denise and sat with her for a few minutes until she fell asleep. Mrs Horgan was in the kitchen when she left. Kate explained she'd call again during the week but that she'd be in surgery until five should she be needed.

Kate returned to the centre, grabbed a sandwich and began her afternoon list. By five she had finished and Mrs Horgan hadn't phoned so she could only assume that Denise was still asleep.

On the way home Kate felt uneasy, but there was little she could do for Denise tonight and suddenly she felt very tired herself. It had been tougher than she had expected to return to surgery today, probably because she'd relaxed over the weekend. It was at times like this that the shadow of the ME taunted her but she knew this fatigue was transitory, nothing like the bone-deep exhaustion of the ME, which used to deplete her so badly.

Before going over to the house, she showered, slipped on fresh, silky, oyster-coloured underwear and pampered herself with a new body cream she'd been keeping for a rainy day. Her hair was a mess so she washed it twice and conditioned it. Just before she dressed she brushed it dry and let it fall in rippling waves over her shoulders.

She pulled on a summer dress with a scooped neckline and a tiny, nipped-in waist. She wondered if she should take something across with her to cook and then decided against it. Had she really thought this through? she wondered as she stood hesitantly at the top of the stairs. Was she about to put herself through the same heartbreak that had followed after Julian . . . and yet, how was she to stop herself?

Then the phone rang and she flew to answer it. 'Kate?' Ben asked softly. 'What's wrong? Something's happened, hasn't it?'

'No, no . . . not really.'

'Are you coming over?'

His voice was low as he said, 'I thought perhaps you'd changed your mind.'

To tell him that she almost had was suddenly inconceivable. 'No,' she lied.

Surprisingly he laughed. 'Kate, I know you by now.'

Did he? Neither of them really knew the other. They both wanted one another— needed one another—but after this, when it was time for her to leave, what then? It was silly to be thinking of that now, after the weekend—silly after she already knew what their love-making had promised.

He said quietly, 'Kate, I've no right to want

184

you the way I do. I can't make you promises. If you stop it here, I'll understand. I won't like it, but I'll understand.'

Perversely, she suddenly knew exactly what she wanted. 'I'm coming over,' she whispered. 'Give me two minutes.'

*　　　*　　　*

Had Kate known how the evening would be, she would never have hesitated. They cooked pasta and salad, and afterwards fell into Ben's huge bed. Their love-making was passionate, almost desperate. She was now taking precautions against falling pregnant and she told him so, but they were too wrapped up in one another's bodies to talk more.

They finally slept, awaking just before midnight to make love again, this time slowly—without the driving ache that had made their earlier passion so intense. And her own response was, this time, free from the shadow of Julian. Love-making with Julian had often left her wondering what it was that rendered such a beautiful act so lacking in intimacy. Not that she'd ever had qualms about his masculinity but perhaps she'd sensed that his first love had invariably come between them—Julian loved Julian—and to her regret she'd never challenged this. Only now, when Ben's passion ignited in her the spirit of true warmth, did she understand how selfless a sexual act could be.

It was bliss to discover each other in the luxury of an empty house, falling asleep in Ben's arms without worrying about time. Kate was aware of the soft brush of the sheet over her skin, the touch of his lips on her forehead and the wonderful security of his strong arms locked about her.

She woke at five, her heart pounding. As if he sensed her fear, he pulled her against him, kissing her sleepily. 'I'm here,' he whispered.

His mouth moved in slow sweeps over her face and neck and breasts. This time, with delightful anticipation, she responded to the passage of his hands as they moved over the soft swell of her hips.

'Did I tell you how beautiful you are?' He slipped his hand to the base of her spine and drew her against him. She gulped for air, her fingertips hot on his body. Her heart beat so rapidly it almost choked her. 'I want you all over again,' he told her raggedly.

'Let me now,' she whispered, as she stroked the smooth, hard muscle beneath her fingers. 'I want to please you . . .'

'Oh, God, Kate, you do—all the time.'

Fulfilment left them shuddering and exhausted. They lay side by side—fingers linked, limbs touching, hearts thudding—and for the next hour she curled into his arms, only half-awake, as the sky grew blue with sunlight.

CHAPTER NINE

Breakfast was taken on the terrace, Ben serving toast and coffee. The sun was warm enough to penetrate the small, fluffy white clouds even at seven-fifteen in the morning—Kate couldn't have wanted more.

She sat at the wrought-iron table across from Ben and breathed in the aroma of coffee, rambling rose and a smooth and sultry cologne as he reached out to hold her hand.

'This is heaven,' she said with a sigh, feeling his fingers tight around her knuckles.

He smiled and her heart leapt again. He looked devastating in a short-sleeved blue shirt, dark linen trousers and a smart and rather jazzy blue and mustard tie. Kate swallowed at the sight of him. Neither of them had bothered to read the newspaper. It lay abandoned on one of the elaborate wrought-iron garden chairs. Kate smiled to herself, amazed at the neglect of what was usually such a necessary part of the morning ritual.

'Will I see you tonight?' Ben was looking at her teasingly, his grey eyes filled with amusement. This was the man who had made such tender and passionate love to her through the night, and here they were, sitting and talking as though they'd known each other for years. That was the way it felt.

'I think I might just have the time,' she teased back.

'I have to collect Caesar after surgery, but I should be back by seven.'

'Have we anything in—shall I stop at the shop for groceries?' Kate frowned.

'No,' he murmured, 'I know exactly what I want for supper. Something smooth and sweet . . . comfort food.' The white tips of his teeth sparkled under his curving lips. 'Haven't you noticed I've acquired rather a sweet tooth lately?'

Kate laughed softly, blushing. 'You know what they say—a sweet tooth is addictive.'

He nodded, the message in his eyes quite clear. 'It's true. I can vouch for it.'

Kate ran her hand along the ridge of his outstretched arm and looked up. He leaned forward and his mouth melted over hers with a kiss of blissful promise.

*   *   *

The normal conventions of family life were suspended during the time the boys were away. Only the constraints of work caused them to limit the hours they spent together.

The twins rang almost every day, though, and—despite Tom missing Lisa—they said they were having a wonderful time. At Ben's suggestion Mrs Howard stayed on with her daughter in Oxford, leaving the house free.

188

In retrospect, Kate couldn't remember seeing a photograph of Paula in Ben's room, but she discovered one in Tom's. It must have been Paula for she held two toddlers, one balanced on each knee. She was a dark and vivacious-looking young woman with intelligent eyes and pale skin like the twins'.

The tragedy of her early death seemed to overwhelm Kate momentarily. She reflected that while she and Ben passed every night in each other's arms Paula's presence hadn't diminished. In a strange way it was a relief to find her photograph. After Kate had studied it she replaced it on Tom's dresser, relieved at least to know what she'd looked like. And she'd guessed correctly. Paula had been a very beautiful woman.

It was also easy, Kate realised, to fall into the habit of knowing that someone was there to embrace and hold and talk to. She was beginning to take for granted the way in which she and Ben were spending their evenings, invariably together, lazing in the sultry August air or just walking Caesar.

Mary Graham hadn't made a visit to the house either, and as for work she was beginning to know her patients better and to enjoy the sense of belonging and usefulness that seemed to be creeping into her life. Her concerns for Denise Markham, though, had deepened. She'd gone to stay with her mother and, it seemed, wasn't recovering from the

189

trauma of her marriage breakdown.

Sheila Dobson took the news of the scan results better than Kate had anticipated. The unpleasant side-effects of her disease had bewildered her, but now that she understood the cause of her problems she appeared resigned to accepting whatever it was her consultant would advise.

Kate had also received Sara Conway's laparoscopy results, and it was a hot August Monday when Sara came in to see her. She sank into the chair, looking pale and tired.

'The symptoms seem to be getting worse.' She sighed, pushing back her short fair hair with a weary gesture. 'My back's a nightmare and my period is giving me hell.'

'We've had the results of the laparoscopy,' Kate explained, concerned at her patient's deterioration in health. 'They indicate ovarian cysts, sometimes termed "chocolate cysts" because of their colour. The displaced endometrium involved with your monthly cycle probably accounts for much of the pain.'

Sara frowned. 'Can these cysts be removed?'

Kate hesitated. 'Yes, they can. Treatment depends on a number of factors and your gynaecologist will discuss the alternatives with you.'

'You mean, something like a hysterectomy?'

Kate nodded. 'That's one alternative, yes.'

'I've always wanted children,' Sara said abruptly. Sensing that she needed to give voice

190

to her suppressed feelings, Kate waited for her to go on. 'I've given everything to Hugh,' Sara faltered, close to tears. 'He's been my baby—I just had to take over, accept the responsibilities and get on with life after he came out of the army. I've coped, God help me, in ways I never thought I could.'

Her voice hardened as she added on a mirthless laugh, 'Every day of my married life I've hoped—dreamed—of a family one day without Hugh's illness wrecking our lives over and over again.' Her body slumped even more in the chair and she looked down at her clenched hands. 'Lots of women would think me ungrateful. I've a lovely home and a good career. No money worries . . .' After a few moments Sara had control of herself again and she looked up, frowning. 'Do you mind me asking how old you are, Kate?'

'I'm thirty-one.'

'And you've never thought about a family?'

Kate nodded. 'Oh, yes, I've thought about it,' she admitted, recalling the bitter disappointment of her dashed hopes for a family with Julian, 'but I'm afraid it just hasn't happened.'

Sara let out a sigh, her shoulders drooping. 'Hugh's forty-seven and I'm thirty-eight—thirty-nine in a couple of months. How can I possibly think of a child now with Hugh the way he is? Even if I conceived how could I divide myself between a sick man and a child?

191

On the face of it, Kate, a hysterectomy should be a blessing.'

Kate sat with her patient a little longer. During the course of their conversation she learned how Sara had been pregnant when Hugh had returned from one of his postings. But she'd miscarried and that had coincided with the first of Hugh's deep depressions. Although Sara had never spoken of the miscarriage before, Kate wondered if this might have caused her to harbour resentment over the years.

When Sara had gone, Angie called into her room. Although Kate was sure Angie couldn't have found out about the weekend she'd spent at Christchurch, some of Angie's questions about how she was finding it to live so close to Ben were rather unsettling. Managing to divert the conversation, Kate breathed a sigh of relief as Angie finally hurried off to her next clinic. Kate found herself thinking about Sara once more. Thirty-nine was not past childbearing age, but even if a baby came along how would the Conways cope with a family and Sara's divided role as breadwinner and nurse?

That evening Kate wondered if she should raise the subject with Ben, but one of a more personal nature surfaced as they stood together in the kitchen, clearing away the supper dishes.

Suddenly she found his arms winding around her. 'Tough day?' he whispered in her ear, his breath fanning her skin.

She nodded, laying her head on his chest as she loved to do. 'I'm on call tonight, too.'

'Damn.' He grinned. 'I wonder if I could bribe Maureen into setting you free for the next couple of weeks while the boys are away?'

'Oh, no way.' Kate laughed softly. 'Two and two is already being made into five.' He crooked an eyebrow and she told him about Angie.

'Idle tongues,' he teased, but as silence fell between them, he frowned down at her. 'Does the prospect of gossip really worry you?'

She shrugged. 'I seem to be surviving. And Angie's a good friend. She could keep a secret—'

'So that's what we are—a secret?' He took her face between his hands and looked into her eyes. 'Kate, I've never asked you—I've never wanted to pry. I know you've been hurt, and I worry. I don't want you to be hurt again.'

'Meaning that hurt is inevitable?'

He pulled her to him and held her close. 'Oh, Kate, sometimes I wonder what I've done . . .'

Kate shook her head determinedly. 'Perhaps what we have is so good because . . . because . . .'

'Because it must come to an end? Is that what you're saying?'

She was silent, staring up at him.

'You're very special to me, Kate. You know

that, don't you?'

She nodded, taking a deep gulp of air. For a moment he stared at her, as if fighting some inner battle. Finally, she broke the silence which seemed to have engulfed them. 'I'm grateful for this—for what we have,' she whispered. 'For every single moment we're together, I'm so very grateful.'

There was a brief pause before he said quietly, 'Kate . . . what do you see as the future for yourself?'

Kate lifted her head and stared at him. 'The future?' She leaned back from his arms and shrugged. 'I'm well now. Sometimes I can't believe I feel so well. Now I can actually think about medicine, about my career.'

'And a family?' He stood and looked at her with a deep frown. 'You'll want children some day, won't you?'

She tried to read his thoughts as she recalled her conversation with Sara today regarding motherhood. 'Yes, I want a family— of course I do—but in view of my background I think that's no surprise, is it?'

Ben's expression changed, but she thought she saw a flash of disappointment in his eyes. But she *did* want a family. He'd experienced fatherhood—knew what it was like to have two gorgeous boys of his own. By the same token, knowing the struggle he'd had, she was under no illusions that he didn't want additional commitments to those he already had. She wasn't blind, either, to the fact he was warning her of the consequences of their brief affair.

'You'll have a wonderful family one day,' he said. 'I just wish it could have been us . . .' He shrugged heavy shoulders and looked at her helplessly. 'I wish I'd met you earlier, Kate. I wish things had been different for us. I wish—Damn it!' He opened his arms, his eyes full of regret. 'Come here,' he groaned, and pulled her towards him. His hands found their way roughly into her hair and his lips were hard on her mouth, searching out her response.

She swallowed on the pain that tore at her heart, knowing he'd told her the simple truth. She'd known what she was doing when she'd begun to love this man. She'd known she'd have to pay a price. And now she was paying it. He'd never lied to her, and for that, at least, she was grateful.

*   *   *

Tessa arrived at the surgery a few days later, coming directly in to see Kate who'd just finished seeing her last patient of the morning. Tessa had recovered physically from the ordeal of the car accident, and as she handed Kate a small white envelope she looked her old self, her blonde hair curling softly about her pretty face.

'It's you I have to thank for being here,' she said, as Kate unsealed the envelope. 'I don't

195

remember much except there were what seemed like explosions all around me and I was shunted forward and the windscreen smashed. After that it all went dark. I didn't even feel much pain. The police said that you crawled into the car before the firemen arrived. If you hadn't got to me then, I don't suppose I'd be here today.'

Kate shrugged lightly. 'It was just lucky that Dr Buchan and I happened to be visiting a patient in the area at the time.' Kate's eyes opened wide as she read the silver-embossed writing on the card. 'Oh, Tessa, how wonderful. You're getting married in December.'

'I've always wanted a Christmas wedding. Rupert thinks I'm crazy, but the accident made us realise what we wanted most out of life. Otherwise . . .' She shrugged. 'Maybe we'd have just drifted on. Both of us have our careers and they seemed to have taken priority for a long while. But Rupert's been wonderful through all this. He's been a tower of strength.'

Suddenly Kate felt her heart quicken as Tessa's words brought back her own despair when Julian had been so swift to abandon her when she'd become ill. If there had ever been any doubt in her mind over the breaking of their engagement, certainly Tessa's remarks had finally made it clear to Kate that their marriage, had it taken place, would surely have been doomed.

196

Managing to smile, Kate leaned forward and kissed Tessa on both cheeks. 'Congratulations to you both,' she said, slipping the invitation to the wedding in her pocket. 'Unfortunately, I shan't be living in Milchester in December, but I shall do my best to attend.'

'Oh!' Tessa exclaimed in surprise. 'I didn't know you were leaving.'

Kate nodded. 'I'm only filling Dr Withycombe's place until his replacement arrives in the autumn.'

Tessa sighed. 'Oh, dear, that is a pity. You seem so right for this practice.'

At that moment there was a knock on the door and Ben appeared, his face brightening as he saw who was in the room. They all talked for a while and Tessa gave Ben one of the invitations too, remarking again on how fortunate she'd been that both Ben and Kate had been in the vicinity the day of the accident and how grateful she was that Kate had taken the swift action she had. When she said how sorry she was to hear that Kate would be leaving, Ben nodded, his gaze coming across to meet Kate's. There was a short silence, then Tessa said that she had to go as she was about to return to Oxford where she'd been recuperating at her parents' home.

After she'd left, Ben sank into the patient's chair. He sat casually, with the ankle of one leg resting on his other knee, fiddling idly with his

197

shoelace. 'She's right, you know,' he said, looking up at Kate. 'You probably saved her life.'

However, Kate was deep in thought, Tessa's comment about the accident reminding her in some vague way of something half-formulated in her mind. 'Ben, when was it that Hugh Conway had his relapse?' she asked hesitantly.

Ben frowned. 'May. Just after you joined us, I believe.'

'And Sara once told me that he always seems to be worse in the spring.' She chewed thoughtfully on her bottom lip. 'Sara also told me that she had a miscarriage years ago. That, too, coincided with one of Hugh's depressive times—again in May.'

'So you're saying his illness may worsen at a certain time of year?' Ben murmured thoughtfully.

'Well, it was Tessa who made me think. While she was recollecting how the accident happened, I, too, remembered the impacts. They were enormous. They seemed to shake the ground, possibly because the motorway is above the cottage and the sound echoes into the small valley beneath.'

Ben nodded. 'Yes, that's right. Hugh leapt out of his chair when it happened and then we both rushed into the garden.'

'And I looked back to see him standing there as we drove away . . .'

'What are you suggesting, Kate?'

'To tell you the truth, I'm not sure. But one word Tessa used—"explosion". The accident did sound like a series of explosions. And Hugh was depressed—you might say, in an extremely sensitive state of mind. What if his illness has something to do with a specific explosion?'

Ben frowned, then nodded slowly. 'Some tangible event that he's repressing?'

'It's possible. Do we know what trouble spots he served in over the years?'

Ben shook his head. 'No. David Bright's not been able to get much out of him.'

'I think David should be told about the miscarriage and Hugh's reaction to those explosions. I think it's important, Ben.'

'All right, I'll get on to him right away. And, Kate . . .'

She slowly brought her attention back and found that he'd come around to stand beside her. Taking her hands, he lifted her to her feet and drew her towards him. 'Where would you like to eat this Saturday?'

She wondered what they'd do if someone came in, and as she thought of it she realised she really didn't care. Laughing softly, she looked up into the face into which she'd gazed for so many mornings as it lay on the pillow beside her. 'Anywhere,' she said on a husky whisper as his lips came down to brush her own.

'The West End.' He grinned. 'Dinner and a

show. We may as well before the boys come home.'

'Done.' She sighed and he kissed her again as footsteps passed by the door and hurried toward Reception.

*   *   *

The weekend in London was fun. Ben took her to cosy little Italian restaurants and wild fringe theatres. They strolled by the river and shopped and talked endlessly. On their way home they ate Sunday lunch at a pub and much later that day, after collecting the dog, they made love in her small bed at The Den, then ambled back hand in hand to the house at midnight under a full and brilliantly silver moon.

*   *   *

On Monday morning Kate was lying warmly wrapped in Ben's arms when the telephone rang. Kate listened sleepily as he answered the call, admiring the strong back and long legs as they moved from under the sheet.

'It's Hugh,' he told her, bending to kiss her good morning. 'He's discharged himself from hospital. No one seems to know where he is. They're just trying to figure out which of the staff saw him last.'

She sat up. 'They haven't told Sara yet?'

200

'No. It's early. Not six yet. They're holding off until I get there and then, if we can't find him . . .' He shrugged. 'I suppose we'll have to.'

'I'd better be with her,' Kate decided, pulling on her robe. 'Will you ring me there?'

He nodded, then reached out to pull her towards him. 'I'll miss you.'

'Me, too. It was a lovely weekend.' She looked up just in time to catch the expression of longing that filled his eyes.

As it was, Kate arrived at the Conways' cottage to find both Sara and Hugh safely together under one roof.

'I was going to telephone Ben,' Sara apologised, as she led Kate into the small sitting room, where Hugh was sitting, unshaven, in one of the armchairs. Sara was still in her bathrobe and Hugh wore a shirt and trousers which both looked as though they'd been crumpled for days in his bedside locker. 'But I thought it was too early in the morning to get him up.'

Hugh, who seemed unaware of the panic he'd caused, suddenly frowned and in a voice that faltered said that he hadn't realised his abrupt departure from the hospital would cause so much concern.

By the time Kate reached Ben on the mobile phone he'd already arrived at Milchester Hospital and had contacted David Bright. Relieved to know that Hugh was safe, Ben told Kate he'd drive straight over.

201

'How is he?' Ben asked when he arrived fifteen minutes later. He stood with Kate in the small hall of the cottage, his face still bearing signs of tiredness, and Kate had to prevent herself from reaching up to smooth away the tiny creases from his eyes.

'He seems to be well enough physically.' Kate shrugged. 'Of course, I'm not able to judge his mental state. He suddenly decided, he said, he wanted to come home, and apparently just walked out of the hospital, after changing in the loo, and caught a taxi.'

'Well, the unit he was in isn't a secure unit— he was there as a voluntary patient.' Ben sighed as he ran a hand through his dishevelled hair. 'But he's shown no signs of wanting to discharge himself before. I wonder why this has happened?'

Kate shook her head. 'I've no idea.'

'Is Sara coping?'

'I've had a word with her and she seems to be handling it all—though it was a shock for her to see the taxi from her bedroom window and Hugh just standing there at five in the morning.'

Ben sighed again, a weary smile on his face. 'Oh, well, I'd better go on in.'

She nodded. 'See you back at surgery.'

He grinned. 'Make sure you eat some breakfast.' Glancing along the hall, he turned back and tilted up her chin. 'Good morning, Dr Ross,' he breathed, kissing her with a

202

tenderness that made her tremble.

The kiss was still tingling on her lips as she drove back to Deer Lane, although by the time she arrived there the early morning traffic was building up and she had to force herself to concentrate.

It took her longer to walk a lethargic Caesar than it did to eat a swift breakfast and repair the damage to her face and hair of the hurried departure from bed that morning. It was almost nine before she arrived at surgery and her first patient had been waiting, rather irritably, for almost half an hour.

As Kate settled herself in her room she wondered how Ben was coping with Hugh Conway. Fearing Ben might have to section him, she wondered whether Hugh's refusal to remain in hospital would signal yet another crisis in the Conways' lives. She was so deep in thought that she looked at Jocylyn blankly for a moment when the receptionist poked her head around the door.

Then the tall, blond figure of Julian appeared behind her and smiled.

CHAPTER TEN

'This gentleman says—' Jocylyn looked both annoyed and bewildered '—that you—he—'

'It's all right, Jocylyn.' Kate walked towards the door. 'Will you please tell my first patient I shall be free in a few seconds?'

Jocylyn nodded, her cheeks red as she cast Julian a doubtful frown on her way out.

Before Kate had time to speak Julian had stepped forward. She just managed to avert her face as he tried to kiss her so that his lips brushed her cheek. 'Kate, how wonderful to see you again.'

'Hello, Julian.'

His blue eyes went over her admiringly. 'You look terrific. Life must be treating you well.'

Kate rested her hand on the open door. 'I'm sorry to seem abrupt, Julian, but I'm running late as it is.'

'Oh, yes, of course.' He cast a glance behind him to the waiting room. 'Actually, I was rather hoping I could take you to lunch.' Kate was so surprised that it must have shown on her face because he added swiftly, 'I'm passing through, you see. One of my clients lives in Altshot, only a few miles away.'

Kate shook her head. 'I shan't have time, Julian—'

'The Red Lion looks promising,' he interrupted her, 'the little pub on the other side of your car-park wall? Surely you'll have an hour to spare between surgeries—for old times' sake?'

Whether it was because she was in a rush to get away or because she was curious to know how Julian had found out she was living in Milchester and what he wanted of her, she found herself agreeing eventually to meet him at one o'clock.

When he'd gone Kate found that she was trembling slightly. Aware that her patients were now almost three quarters of an hour behind time, she had to make a concerted effort to put Julian out of her mind. She lifted the telephone and asked Jocylyn to explain to each patient before they came in that she'd been unavoidably detained before arriving at surgery.

She made a personal apology to each patient as well, and was relieved halfway through the morning to discover that two mid-morning patients had cancelled. That brought her back on schedule by midday.

As the time crept closer to one o'clock she began to think that Julian might have been an apparition and that she'd imagined it all. However, when Jocylyn came to her room after her last patient and commented that Kate's early morning visitor had rudely insisted on seeing her straight away, Kate was left in no doubt that it was Julian.

Just as Jocylyn was saying how unbelievably thoughtless some people could be, Ben appeared and, smiling, sauntered across to Kate's desk.

'Oh, well, if there's nothing else . . .?' Jocylyn asked, smiling at Ben.

'No, nothing,' Kate said gratefully. 'And I'm sorry about this morning.'

'Obviously thought he was the cat's whiskers,' commented Jocylyn dryly as she went out.

Ben smiled curiously. 'Sounds intriguing. Anyone I know?'

Kate felt her heart sink. She had no reason to lie and yet she was reluctant to admit that Jocylyn was referring to Julian. She was even more reluctant to explain that she had inadvisedly—now she'd thought about it— agreed to go to lunch with him. 'It was Julian, as a matter of fact,' she said quietly.

'Oh, I see.' He arched one eyebrow. 'Were you expecting him?'

'No, in fact, I can't think how he has my address. Certainly I never gave it to him.'

'Have you any idea what he wants?' His tone was casual, but she felt a distinct coolness in the air.

'Well, apparently he's passing through, meeting a client . . .'

'Or perhaps he was curious. About you.'

Kate felt her cheeks redden. 'Perhaps. But it

seems unlikely.' She sighed as she sat back in her chair. 'Though he did ask if I could have lunch with him and, rather foolishly, I've agreed.'

He lifted his dark brows and frowned at her. 'Well, I suppose you know what you're doing. Look, I've some news for you,' he said shortly. 'Hugh's much better—slightly confused as to how he left hospital perhaps, but his overriding desire was suddenly to get home as quickly as possible to talk to Sara. Try to straighten things out in his mind.'

Kate realised she'd forgotten about Hugh. Rather guiltily she listened as Ben explained that David Bright had had several extremely rewarding therapy sessions with Hugh in the previous week and it had been a sudden clarity of mind, which had evolved over the weekend, that had brought Hugh Conway to leave the hospital.

'On the whole,' Ben continued, 'I think that, far from reaching a crisis, he's started to come to terms with the past. It's early days yet, but . . .' He shrugged. 'Anyway, David Bright is seeing him this afternoon. I've squared things with the hospital so, hopefully, we may see a new chapter in the Conways' lives.'

'How was Sara?' Kate asked as they walked slowly into the hall.

'She hasn't had time to adjust yet, but I think she'll be fine.' Ben frowned as he looked ahead. 'Is this your lunch date arriving?'

207

Kate followed his gaze. A city-suited figure was striding towards them, a good-looking blond man slightly shorter than Ben.

'Ben,' Kate said, 'this is Julian Francis. Julian—Dr Buchan.'

'Hello, there.' Julian's voice was smooth and friendly. Ben nodded and shook hands, but he soon made an excuse to leave. Kate watched him go, aware of a sinking sensation inside her at his abrupt attitude.

'Back for two,' she called to Hilly as she and Julian walked through Reception.

'But that barely gives us time to talk,' Julian complained as they walked outside into the sunshine.

Kate smiled. 'Well, this really is like old times, isn't it?' she murmured dryly.

*   *   *

It was just two when Kate and Julian emerged from the Red Lion into a day that was now overcast. She hadn't tasted the sandwich and orange juice he'd bought her and had listened inattentively to his conversation. In fact, all the meeting had served to do was to annoy her. She had no interest in the fact he'd broken up with his girlfriend or that he no longer spent his weekends aboard his beloved motor boat. Why she'd ever agreed to meet him, she couldn't think. If she'd been in her right senses that morning she'd have guessed it had been her previous practice manager who'd been persuaded by Julian to pass on her address.

They stopped at a flashy red sports car and Julian took hold of her arm. 'I'm thinking of staying in Milchester overnight,' he told her. 'Perhaps we could have dinner. And then you could tell me all about yourself.'

'Julian, we've absolutely nothing to say to one another,' she protested, realising he wasn't about to release her.

'I know I behaved badly,' he admitted sourly, 'but things have changed now and I realise how much I miss you in my life.' He narrowed his eyes at her. 'Are you involved with someone else?'

Kate winced at the pressure he put on her wrist. 'Let go of me, Julian.'

She was beginning to panic when a large hand came down on Julian's arm. 'What the devil do you think you're doing?' Ben growled angrily.

Kate pulled away her arm. 'Julian is just leaving,' she said, taking a breath. 'I don't think we've anything more to say to one another.'

Glaring at Kate, he unlocked his car and sank into the driver's seat, slamming the door after him. The unnecessary roar of the engine caused Kate to wince. Ben took her elbow, guiding her away from the irritable swerve of the vehicle.

'Are you all right?' Ben looked down at her.

'Yes,' she gulped, rubbing her wrist. 'Sorry about that.' Kate was angry at herself now. 'Heaven knows why I agreed to lunch.'

He looked at her sharply. 'Obviously you had your reasons.' And before she could reply he had turned to stride towards the surgery. Kate followed him in silence. Hilly and Lesley were on duty behind the desk, but she didn't pause to look at them. Once in her room her heart slowed and she sat down for a moment, confused by Ben's attitude and angry with herself for the way she'd handled Julian's visit. Still, there was no point in repeatedly going over what had happened. She'd been foolish to go out with him, yes, but it was over now. And if there had ever been any doubts in her heart as regards her feelings towards Julian, his brief appearance in her life had at least resolved those!

By the end of the afternoon the pile of records on her desk made her realise how many summer coughs and colds had comprised her busy surgery. Her eyes went tiredly to the Victorian penny she'd found at Christchurch. Running over its rough edges with her finger, she recalled the sensation of swimming in the cool, clear water beside Ben. He'd felt strong and safe beside her and they'd come to know each other so much better since then. She just hoped that Julian's unfortunate appearance in their lives would be quickly forgotten.

And it was—to an extent. They ate dinner

and talked about the Conways and the boys coming home as if the incident with Julian had never happened. And yet Julian's absence from the conversation made everything else sound superficial.

That night she slept fitfully in Ben's arms and woke with a feeling of uncertainty, the ghosts of Julian and Paula feeling oddly close. Perhaps it was this feeling that also sharpened the edge to their conversation later in the day.

'I had a call from one of the practices in Yorkshire,' Kate explained as they drank coffee in the staffroom during the afternoon break. 'They've offered me a partnership before Christmas—sooner than I'd expected, really.'

Ben was silent, raising his head to stare at her. 'I see.'

Kate wished she hadn't mentioned it. Not here. Not like this, where it seemed impossible to talk with the buzz of staff conversation in the background. 'I'll fit in with whatever you want, of course, depending on when your colleague from South Africa arrives.' Her voice sounded practical and businesslike, but inside she was hurting, hurting desperately. And yet what choice was there? She had to go. They both knew this had to happen. She *had* to tell him.

'I'll find out. Let you know.' He looked down at his mug, the lines and grooves on his face deepening.

211

'All right. Yes.'

They both sat in stony silence.

She was the first to break it. 'Ben, it had to happen eventually. We both knew that.'

He looked up again, his face seeming older and more haggard, and her heart clenched. 'I just wish it wasn't now,' he said miserably. 'It's funny. I'd put it all to the back of my mind—blocked it out, I suppose.' He gave a bitter laugh. 'The past has rather caught up with us over the last few days, hasn't it?'

She nodded, tears springing to the corners of her eyes. She knew exactly what he meant.

*   *   *

On the Friday before the boys were due home Kate prepared a special supper, a candlelit meal with a good wine and chicken cooked in herbs. Although it had been Ben's week of late extras, he arrived home at six-thirty in a squall of wind and summer rain.

Caesar made his usual fuss and Kate called out that she was in the kitchen. She was wearing a blue, ankle-length, gypsy dress. It swirled coolly around her legs and she'd tied her hair back with a scarf.

Without a word he pulled her into his arms. 'You look beautiful,' he whispered, and she tilted her face to his lips. 'I need you now, Kate . . .' He slid the scarf from her hair and buried his face in the soft silkiness. 'Oh, Kate,

212

time's gone too quickly.'

She felt a flash of pain. 'Yes, my love, too quickly,' she murmured weakly.

He folded her into his arms. She could feel the beat of his heart, feel the heat of his body burn into hers. Suddenly she wanted to let him know how she felt, to say the things she'd prevented herself from saying every night as she'd lain alongside him, secure in his arms. Just as she was despairing that she'd never be able to say those things, he held her gently away from him.

'Kate, there are things I should tell you . . . things I should explain . . .' he muttered bleakly. 'It didn't seem to matter before. But now . . . I can't let you go, without knowing why, knowing things I couldn't bring myself to admit.'

'Tell me later,' she whispered. He nodded and pulled her to her feet, taking her in his arms and holding her for a long time.

Their love-making was urgent, almost primitive. Their release was bound up with something indefinable, fulfilment gained in aching climax that rocked both of them as they shuddered back down to earth.

'Oh, Kate, I've taken all this for granted,' he groaned afterwards as they lay in each other's arms. 'I don't know what to say.'

'Don't say anything,' she murmured, and he brought her against him, laying her head on his chest and wrapping her in his arms. He sifted

213

his fingers through her hair and kissed the top of her head. She felt him heave a sigh.

'Paula was having an affair,' he told her in the darkness, expelling a long, shuddering breath. 'She was with him when she died. They both loved sailing, something she'd grown very fond of in South Africa. I thought perhaps the relationship might burn itself out—at least, I thought she might change her mind. We'd talked of divorce, you see. She'd gone away to think about things . . . though what we'd had in South Africa we'd never seemed to manage to regain here . . .'

'Oh, Ben . . . I'm so sorry.' She pressed a kiss on his chest. 'Did the boys know, do you think?' She recalled Toby asking her all those questions on the first day she'd met him. He'd wanted to know if she remembered her parents. Had he clearer memories of Paula than anyone supposed?

Ben hesitated above her. 'I think they sensed things were wrong, yes. They were young, only four, but some of it must have registered.' He squeezed her arm. 'That's what was so unfair, so tragic. And afterwards I was determined I'd never risk their happiness again.'

She understood him now. And her heart ached for him. 'They love you, Ben. You've been a wonderful father.'

'I've tried,' he muttered, his voice rumbling in his chest, 'but I still feel I've failed. I can't

214

replace Paula in their lives and I haven't provided them . . . with a woman's kind of loving.' He tilted her face up to him. 'Yet I've tried to do everything in my power to make them happy.'

She nodded, knowing it was true, knowing that however much she loved him their lives had been destined from the start to take different paths.

'I'm sorry, darling,' he whispered, smoothing kisses into her hair. 'It would have been different for us if I hadn't had the boys. You know that, don't you?'

She reached up to kiss him, murmuring against his lips to stop him from speaking, drawing her hands across the broad width of his naked shoulders and loving every inch of skin and bone, knowing that while their time lasted she'd settle for any measure of love that he could give her.

*   *   *

It was in the early hours of the morning when they woke, spent and exhausted. The ebony sky, visible through the window, was studded with tiny, glimmering stars. Kate moaned softly as she eased her naked body under the sheet into the curve of Ben's body beside her, finding the circle of his arms with an instinct that aroused her from her drugged sleep.

She turned to look at his face, loving the

215

strong, firm features, the long nose and high cheeks. She was tempted to run her fingers across the pillow but didn't—her pleasure was too great in just looking. But then, as if he'd known she was watching him, his eyes flicked open and he smiled.

'What are you thinking?' His voice was rough with drowsiness.

She smiled. 'That the candles will be burnt down.'

He laughed softly and moved close to kiss her, his lips seeking yet another response from her body. 'We'll light some more.'

'When?'

'Oh, in a moment, when we go down to see what's left of our dinner.'

She squirmed into the warmth of his chest and drew her hands across its soft wiriness, knowing that to leave the bed would be impossible.

He smiled above her in the darkness. 'Or we can just stay like this.'

As moonlight slowly flooded the room, she lifted her face and he kissed her.

*   *   *

Ben chose an overcast Sunday to collect the boys. Rain threatened as he left and Kate kissed him goodbye. She wondered how their lives would change once the boys were home. He'd insisted he'd come across to The Den when he returned and that they'd continue to meet, but Kate knew that it wouldn't be easy to arrange.

As Kate was on call she walked Caesar and then went across to The Den to open the windows to air it. She was paged mid-morning and the call was from Mrs Horgan, Denise Markham's mother. When Kate arrived at the bungalow Mrs Horgan was waiting at the door.

'She's in bed,' said the woman with a sigh of exasperation. 'I made her lie down, but I don't know what to do with her. She's in tears all the time and has lost interest in everything, even keeping the house clean.'

In the small bedroom Denise lay on the bed, her eyes swollen and puffed. Kate sat on the bed and drew Denise's hand from her eyes. Despair and desperation filled her once pretty face, and it was only after a good deal of gentle persuasion that she began to talk, explaining that Gareth had refused to let the boys return home and that custody would be decided through the courts.

'I . . . I just can't seem to cope.' Denise sobbed. 'Without Gareth it was terrible. Now the boys have gone . . .' She looked helplessly at Kate as though she were in physical pain.

Kate was reluctant to prescribe an antidepressant but felt that she had to, at least for a temporary period. Finally, she arranged with Mrs Horgan, who had a car, to bring her daughter in to surgery the following day, where Kate would set up some counselling. Kate also wanted to ask Rupert to contact Gareth Markham. She hadn't given up hope that some kind of compromise could be struck out of court.

Later that day the phone was ringing as Kate returned home and she had to run up the stairs to catch it. 'We thought you were coming, too,' Toby's young voice announced. 'You could have snorkelled again, only you'd be better at it this time.'

Kate's heart squeezed in a pang of affection. 'Someone had to look after the dog,' she joked.

'Have you seen Lisa?' Tom asked, taking the phone from his brother. 'She said she'd write.'

Kate said she hadn't, although it wasn't quite the truth. She'd seen Lisa but she'd been with another boy in town. Finally she was transferred to Ben.

'I'll see you about elevenish in the morning,' he murmured, and she wondered if the boys were safely out of earshot as he added, 'I've missed you.'

After a restless night alone in her own bed she woke up early, missing the solid form curled against her. The sun streamed in through the window and she made herself toast, recalling their shared breakfasts eaten on the terrace. Distractedly she fed Caesar, who'd come over from the house the previous night and stayed with her, his comforting presence a salutary reminder of the changes about to take place in her life.

CHAPTER ELEVEN

At work that morning, Kate asked Rupert if he could shed any light on the situation with the Markham children. He told her he felt Gareth Markham would co-operate with a social worker and, encouraged, Kate made several calls, setting in motion the first steps toward a line of communication.

Once in her room her thoughts drifted to Ben and the boys, who'd be travelling back from Christchurch.

As she opened her morning post she found herself looking at a letter regarding Sheila Dobson's recent surgery. She was relieved to read that because of early detection the operation to remove the tumour had been successful.

Halfway through the morning Tina brought in coffee, and a few seconds after she'd gone the door opened again. Kate expected to see her next patient, but a tall, familiar figure entered and her heart leapt. Ben closed the door quietly and hugged her to him, a shudder going through them both as he kissed her.

'Good trip?' she managed to whisper

eventually.

He nodded. 'It's better to be back.' He looked very handsome, with his black hair brushed back from his face and his tall figure clad in a crisp white shirt and dark trousers.

'Boys all right?' she asked.

'Fine. Can't wait to see you.'

'I've missed them,' she admitted. 'Are they at home?'

He nodded, pushing back her hair from her face. 'Mrs Howard is due back from Oxford at lunchtime. No doubt she'll sort them out.'

'Did Toby mention school?' she asked as he let her go.

He sighed. 'No, but I found a letter waiting for me today from the head. Unless Toby can come up with a convincing argument for his behaviour, some measure must be taken against him before the beginning of term.'

'You mean expulsion?' Kate frowned.

He shrugged. 'I wouldn't rule it out. Unfortunately, Toby's silence is taken as an admission of guilt. I gave him the letter to read, hoping he'd be more forthcoming about what had happened at school, but he just seems to have retreated into his shell. Obviously I can't do anything if he won't confide in me.'

Kate paused as voices outside the door grew louder. 'There must be something we can do, Ben. I'd stake everything I own that Toby is shielding someone.'

He sighed, lifting despairing shoulders. 'But who?' Then he managed a slow smile as he reached out and squeezed her hand. 'Anyway, I'd better get on. Come for supper this evening. The boys made me promise to ask.'

She nodded and he kissed her briefly, their eyes meeting. She watched his tall figure disappear, knowing that yet again her feelings for him had deepened, but no matter what she did now it was only a question of time before she had to face their parting.

*　　　*　　　*

To Kate's surprise, Denise arrived for her appointment and explained she'd finally come to a decision. Having returned to her own house this morning, she was determined to try to adjust to her circumstances in the hope that Gareth would return the boys. Encouraged by Kate's news, too, she agreed to counselling and a meeting with the social worker.

Kate gradually began to unwind as she drove home that night. The lights spilled out from the house, the front door was open and a bike was propped against the fence. And as she climbed from the car Tom and Toby ran to greet her, both hugging her as she struggled to get to her feet.

They were so eager to tell her about the holiday that she almost had to referee the conversation during supper. Ben grinned at

221

her from the other side of the table, his eyes full of their secret language, making her glow inside.

The sensitive subject of school and Toby's suspension was carefully avoided, and by the time they'd finished the meal it was late. Afterwards, Kate sat with Ben on the terrace while Tom phoned Lisa and Toby watched a video he'd bought. Mrs Howard had decided to take an early night and so they sat alone together in the dusk, with only Caesar lying quietly at their feet.

As the last of the light faded he leaned across the table to take hold of both her hands. 'Kate, I'll miss you tonight. Miss having you by my side . . .'

She nodded. 'I'll miss you, too.'

He lifted his eyebrows. 'What are the chances of me chucking pebbles at your window, do you think?'

She laughed softy. 'Not if you want to wake up for six.'

He pulled a face. 'I'll take a rain check, then. For Saturday night?' He brought her hand to his mouth and kissed each finger tenderly, before raising his eyes to meet hers with such a look of tender longing that, absurdly, she wanted to cry.

*   *   *

At the end of the week Josh Neilson faxed

from South Africa, explaining he'd be arriving in England in a month's time. Kate knew that this heralded the end of her term as locum at Milchester and, much as she tried to put leaving Ben and the boys from her mind, it was a thought that was constantly with her.

At work, Ben told her that Hugh Conway continued to improve, remarking that this was due in part to Kate's suggestion that his anxiety possibly originated from a specific incident involving a bomb blast. The particular incident had been identified during a session with David Bright, and Hugh was now receptive to further therapy. Sara, meanwhile, had opted for a hysterectomy, hopeful now that she and Hugh would be able to live fuller and more reconciled lives.

Then, one warm September evening, shortly after surgery had finished, Kate heard from Peter Frost. 'I'm at my dad's . . . in London,' he told her hesitantly over the phone. 'Dad said I had to tell you what happened at school as he says I can stay here now and I don't have to come back to Milchester.'

'Has this anything to do with being bullied at school, Peter?' Kate asked, remembering what Tom and Lisa had told her that day in the garden.

There was silence and Kate fully expected Peter to hang up. But he didn't.

'Toby was the only one who stuck up for me,' Peter explained. 'Then this prefect started on him too, making out it was Toby who started the fight. I took the money because it was the only way I could get back at the prefect, only it all went wrong and Toby got the blame.'

'Was it the other boy's money that fell out of your pocket when I was examining your knee?' Kate asked.

'Yes,' Peter admitted. 'I wanted to tell you before, but I was too afraid.'

Finally, she spoke to Peter's father. He said he intended to put matters right with the authorities in the hope that Peter would now be able to settle with him in London, but first he wanted to make sure that Toby wasn't blamed for something he hadn't done.

Eager to tell Ben the news, Kate hurried to his room. As the door was ajar she walked in, and he looked up from the paperwork that lay on the desk in front of him. Her heart leapt with a surge of love as he gave her his lazy smile.

She sat down and explained, and an expression of such relief crossed his face that she realised just how much toll the worry had taken over the months. His body visibly relaxed and he gave a long, heartfelt sigh, his lids fluttering down onto his cheeks. 'Oh, God, Kate, that's wonderful news.'

'I was so sure it had to be something like that,' she murmured.

'But why wouldn't Toby confide in me?' His

grey eyes went over her, searching for answers. 'Why has it taken you to make this whole damn nightmare go away? Where am I going wrong?'

She reached out to touch his arm. 'You haven't gone wrong, my darling. It's just that children often find it easier to talk to people outside the family circle. Peter finally talked to his father, but only because he hadn't seen him for years. Don't you remember when you were younger, having someone older to tell all your worries to?'

Ben shrugged. 'Yes, I suppose so. But Toby knew there was a risk of expulsion.' He shook his head uncomprehendingly. 'That's no joke, Kate.'

She nodded. 'All the more reason to admire Toby's loyalty.'

He was silent for a while. Then he frowned. 'I don't suppose any of the boys who were bullied were keen to say what was happening. It could still be going on, for all we know. Well, this particular individual's reign of terror has come to an end. I shall see to that myself.' His face was white with anger as he looked at her and sighed. 'Oh, Kate, I'm sorry to be so cross, but it's just so damned unfair. This wretched business has even cast a shadow over us. There's been so little time . . .'

'Time enough,' she murmured softly, 'for a happy ending for Toby.'

It was a misty, warm September's morning when Maneka Sarkar gave birth to her healthy six-pound-five-ounce baby, three weeks prematurely, in Milchester Hospital. Kate was in Reception, talking to Bal Chandra, when Sanjay arrived at the surgery.

'And we have had a letter to say that we have been allocated new housing near Heathrow,' Sanjay told Kate and Bal, who shook his hand in turn and congratulated him.

'Maneka's only disappointment was that she couldn't use the birthing pool,' Sanjay remarked with a wide grin. 'It was occupied at the time.'

'Then better luck with your next one,' Bal joked, his white smile flashing at Sarkar.

'Never, Dr Chandra! Not for a long time!' Sanjay raised his hands in horror. 'I am a nervous wreck after this.'

They all laughed. As Sanjay was thanking them for the courtesy with which they'd treated his wife, Mary Graham walked in. Kate returned her greeting and, as Bal was saying goodbye to Sanjay, she watched the petite brunette walk hurriedly towards Ben's room.

When Angie arrived for her afternoon clinic she popped into Kate's room, commenting that she'd just passed Mary Graham and Ben in the car park, climbing into the Mercedes.

Kate had been hoping to talk to Ben during

the lunch-hour as their meetings of late had been held at dead of night when everyone else in the house was fast asleep. Ben came over to The Den—not to throw pebbles at the window, as he had once teased, but to let himself in with a key. They made love, aware of the dangers of discovery and the swiftly passing hours that meant he must return to the house before dawn. Even then, Kate was anxious that one of the boys might wake. Today, a Monday, she hadn't managed to see him before surgery and she'd begun to wonder if something had happened at home.

As it was, he had, according to Angie, gone out with Mary Graham. Kate recognised what she was feeling as jealousy. She despised herself for it, but it was true. Wasn't it possible that Mary Graham's presence would feature more in Ben's life after she herself had gone?

Angie leaned back in the patient's chair and tilted her head curiously as she studied Kate's expression. 'When did you first know?' she asked quietly, and Kate, coming back to the present, frowned.

'Know? Know what?'

Angie smiled ruefully. 'That you'd fallen for him. Was it love at first sight, or when you moved in to The Den, or when you went to Christchurch on that supposedly secret weekend of yours?'

Kate blushed. 'You know about that?'

Angie nodded, still grinning. 'Phil saw Toby

227

in town. And boys will be boys. Toby and Tom seem to think you're a permanent fixture in their father's life.'

Kate was astonished. 'I had no idea they thought that—but it's not true, Angie. I'm leaving Milchester. The end of the month, actually.'

Angie's jaw dropped. 'But, Kate, you're in love with him, aren't you?'

Again Kate was lost for words, but she couldn't hope to deceive Angie—or herself—any longer. Miserably she nodded.

Angie leaned forward, crossed her arms on the desk and frowned. 'Then, what's the problem, Kate? Are you afraid of being hurt again after Julian?'

'Yes, I suppose that does come into it, but I thought I could avoid becoming too involved because neither of us wanted commitments—at least, I thought I didn't.' She looked at Angie helplessly. 'But the closer it comes to leaving, the more I realise I don't want to go.'

'So don't!' Angie exclaimed. It's simple. If you love each other—'

'Angie, you don't understand.' Kate sighed. 'He has everything in his life he needs. Family, home, career . . . friends. And Mary Graham.'

Angie spluttered. 'She doesn't seem to have had a look-in while you've been around. Look, does Ben *know* how you feel?'

Kate bit her lip. 'No— Yes— Oh, Angie, I don't know.'

'In other words, he assumes you *want* to hare off and lose yourself for ever in the depths of the countryside?'

Kate shrugged. 'He knows I've arranged a job in the Dales to go to, yes.'

'Well, then!' Angie lifted her hands. 'It's clear he's too proud to ask you to stay and you're too proud to tell him you don't want to leave.'

'It isn't just pride, Angie.' Kate sighed frustratedly. 'There are other considerations. The boys, for instance—'

'But you adore those boys. And they adore you,' Angie broke in emphatically. 'Oh, Kate, don't leave Milchester without telling Ben how you really feel.'

Kate stared at her friend. She wondered if it was just wishful thinking that if she did open her heart she'd find out how he really felt. Then the sensible, logical, little voice inside her reminded her that if he'd wanted to he could have dissuaded her from leaving weeks ago!

No, it was no use believing in fantasies. He'd made it plain he had no intention of entering into a deeper relationship after Paula, and yet here she was, wishing and hoping for something that just couldn't be. Life simply wasn't as straightforward as Angie declared it to be. Oh, that it were!

Kate looked at her friend and sighed. 'Thanks for listening,' she said gratefully.

'But I still haven't changed your mind?' Angie raised her eyebrows.

Kate shook her head and smiled. 'No,' she said quietly. 'It's settled, Angie, I'm afraid. I'm going.'

*   *   *

Not only did Kate dread the time when she would have to say the final goodbye, but as the weeks passed by she found herself rehearsing the moment over and over again in her mind, knowing that even if she put on a brave face her intention to leave without tears would be thwarted.

Fate, however, took a hand in the outcome. On the Wednesday before the weekend she was due to leave Ben received a call from his mother to say that his father had been taken ill. The call came in the middle of the night and Ben and the boys drove to Christchurch immediately, without waking her. He left word with Mrs Howard to say that he'd telephone as soon as he had news.

On Friday he rang and explained that his father had been taken into hospital after a heart attack, asking if it was possible for her to remain a few days longer before leaving Milchester.

She'd agreed she would try before their conversation was interrupted by the twins who wanted to speak to her. She managed to keep her composure, but by the time she replaced the receiver she'd made up her mind. Much as she yearned to see Ben and the boys one last time, she would leave, as she'd arranged, on Saturday. She was exhausted with hiding her feelings, pretending she didn't feel agonised by it all. Perhaps it was just as well it was ending this way, she told herself. And she certainly wasn't going to haggle about it over the phone. Whatever it was she'd been going to say, she'd say it in a letter.

Writing, of course, made it no less difficult. She discovered this as she wrote endless versions, screwing them up and throwing them in the bin. It was easier to write lies, to make excuses, but with each word there was a fresh grief, a realisation this was the end. The absolute end.

Finally, she settled for a few apologetic, grateful lines to Ben, hoping his father would be well and saying how much she'd enjoyed her months here, then wrote twice as many cheerful, loving lines to the boys.

Wrapping up heartbreak in carefully chosen phrases was perhaps marginally less painful. And no one saw the tears.

That, at least, she was grateful for.

CHAPTER TWELVE

Klysdale Practice boasted a team of four doctors and was set in the rugged, breathtaking countryside. Kate knew she would be happy with her change of environment. The London area, she'd reasoned, had occupied the greater part of her life and it was time for change.

However, the minute she arrived she recognised the fact she'd been running away. Her natural environment was the town and City. She was attuned to the crowded streets, the burdens of chaos and frenetic energy. Her natural springboard had been the inner city and commuter towns like Milchester, a microcosm of urban life. Could she change? she wondered in moments of panic.

The eternal green spaces and extraordinary beauty of the Dales sometimes frightened her as the City never had. They seemed to be too beautiful, too rich and generous to be part of her existence. And, of course, her surroundings only enhanced the barrenness inside her, the meaningless existence that she led without Ben and the boys.

She would only allow herself to acknowledge this fear on her darker days, and even then she'd eke out her pain in small measures, shedding tears in ashamed, stifled moments when she was utterly alone.

Most days she went into work with her façade of normality intact. Everyone tried to make her feel welcome. Thank God, she thought often, they can't see the alien inside me, the soulless being who inhabits this body.

Although the doctors of the practice had agreed there should be a month's trial period before her final agreement of partnership, she determined to make Klysdale her new home. Her small cottage, organised temporarily for her by the practice secretary, was adequate for her first few weeks. Perhaps in time, she told herself, she'd find somewhere more to her liking.

She doubled her efforts to understand her patients' problems and the rural way of life of the close-knit farming community. Wondering if it was because the change from Milchester was so great—the pace slower, the patients from farms and villages of an ancient England—she began to accept missing, on a daily basis, a man and his sons who were never far from her thoughts.

There was another source of heartbreak, too. She received no word from Ben. What made the silence worse was a postcard from the boys. They'd both scrawled messages on the flip side of a picture of the cricket pavilion, the place she'd discovered with Toby in her early days in Milchester. They said they missed her and that touched her beyond belief. But there was nothing from their father. No letter. No call.

Gradually she reconciled herself to the fact he must have been content to accept her decision to leave while he was away. This alternately tore her apart and reassured her. She'd been right in accepting it was the end, yet it wounded her afresh when she allowed herself to dwell on it.

*   *   *

Two months after her departure from Milchester, Kate finally stopped watching for the morning post and rushing to the phone each time it rang.

A letter from Angie, however, brought news that Ben's father had recovered from the heart attack, and for that Kate was thankful. But her heart seemed heavier by the day as she looked out over the brooding, crouching hills of the picturesque landscape.

Life, she had discovered, went on. The weeks passed and she was surviving on a diet of hard work and determination to make the best of what she had. The bouts of loneliness were worse when she wasn't working so she found herself at the surgery long after normal hours, burying herself in paperwork.

Then, one heart-piercingly beautiful Saturday—one that she hadn't volunteered duty for because she'd decided she really must begin to look for somewhere more permanent to live—she woke to a morning that might have been stolen from summer. The hills were green and gold and seemed to glow against a clear blue sky.

She'd made a list of places she had to visit—the one letting agency in Klysdale and the estate agent. She was toying with the idea of buying a place in the village. She'd seen one or two renovated cottages, but had dismissed them previously. She hadn't the heart to go looking for a future. But now it was time. She had either to make her stand against the misery that had oppressed her or give in. And she was a fighter. The ME had taught her that. And, thank God, she'd won.

With no morning surgery to attend, she dressed in jeans and a sweater, casually tied back her hair in a ponytail and slipped on sneakers. Then she left the cottage to walk into Klysdale.

At the brow of the hill Kate stopped to watch the scene that greeted her eyes, wondering if she'd ever get used to cars and bicycles and pedestrians who seemed to be moving at a snail's pace. A small shaft of nostalgia shot through her as she thought of Milchester's congested precincts. She stood where she was for a moment, the pang of remembrance engulfing her as she thought of The Den and the boys on their bikes and Ben's tall figure crossing the lawns from the house.

Then she forced it back, took a breath and cleared her mind. It was a process she was used to now—an almost foolproof way of crash-landing back to reality. She reached out to steady herself, took another breath and marched down the hill.

For some reason she turned left where she should have turned right. Klysdale was a funny little village, which had a maze of small streets, and occasionally she lost herself. She knew the letting agency was crammed between a souvenir shop and a bakery, and the aroma of hot bread caused her to make a diversion back to where she should have started.

As she looked along the narrow lane that led back to the main road she blinked, staring at a face which had sprung, it seemed, from her imagination. She was used to the images now, but they came mostly at night. When it was more difficult to keep them at bay. When all her dreams were of Ben.

But this was daytime, a clear, bright, crisp morning, free of the shadows of night and their despairing illusions. Certain she was hallucinating, Kate turned back the way she'd come. She didn't know why. Perhaps it was just too painful to walk past a perfect stranger who'd remind her of Ben.

And then she heard her name being called. And then she was turning. And then she was running. Running as fast as she could, with her heart pounding, her eyes blinking with tears

236

but with a new certainty.

This was real. No vision or illusion.

She was running towards him, and he towards her. Blood rushed through her ears, making her head pound. All clarity went. She was crying and laughing and choking all at the same time. Finally she was in his arms, being held against his solid strength. She lifted her face to be kissed, her hands gripping the tall, dark figure in jeans and jumper who scooped her off her feet and swung her around and around, kissing her until she felt she had no breath left in her body. All her breath and energy fused into a gasp of utter relief, soothing such a deep ache that no words could express how she felt.

It was Ben, finally, who spoke, peeling her away from him as they stood in the tiny, cramped lane in a place where neither of them should be and were. His voice was the same deep, rich tone, the same reverberating sound that made her heart break with joy.

'Oh, Kate . . . Kate.' He hugged her hard, shuddering and holding her tighter. For minutes they stood clinging together as the world revolved around them. She didn't want him to see her face so she pushed it against his chest, closing her eyes against her tears as she listened to the wonderfully familiar pounding of his heart.

Little by little, Kate's breath came back. Ben drew his hand over her hair and pulled her face up to his, wiping the salty moisture from her cheeks with his thumbs.

'Sorry,' she mumbled ashamedly.

'So you should be.'

'I'm just a useless blubberer.' She gulped, trying to focus through the veil of warm tears.

'Blubber all you like. But never run away from me again.' His voice was tender, rebuking, puzzled. She shook her head, staring up into his sad grey eyes.

'But I thought it was what you wanted. And I couldn't face a goodbye.'

'There never should have been a goodbye.' He shook her gently, staring into her eyes. 'Oh, Kate, I've missed you so much. These months have been hell. I shouldn't ever have let you go. I was insane.' Hungrily his mouth searched hers, seeking out her response.

She eased herself away breathlessly. 'I don't understand. I haven't heard . . . I thought it was what you wanted. I thought—'

'No, damn it! Of course it wasn't what I wanted.' He looked pleadingly into her eyes. '*This* is what I want. I want you with me always. I want a life and a future with you. God knows, I've paid for not saying it before. I've paid for being so blind, for being such a fool. I love you, Kate.'

She stared at him, her fingers afraid to touch him. In case he wasn't real. In case what she was hearing wasn't real. Perhaps the ground she was standing on wasn't real.

Perhaps this was all in her mind.

'Kate, listen to me.' He put his hands on her shoulders, stroking them and then running his palms down to her wrists, which he gripped with a gentle pressure as if she might run away. A sigh erupted from his body like a groan of controlled pain.

'Kate, I love you. I love you with all my heart, and I'd give everything to put back the clock. After Paula, I was blind and deaf and wounded and I couldn't share my life—couldn't see beyond the straightjacket I'd imposed on myself. And it wasn't just the boys—that was partly an excuse. I didn't want to be hurt again, to be destroyed again.

'And then I met you. I saw how vulnerable and how brave you'd been and were. I fell in love with you from the first moment . . .' He bent to kiss her open mouth, gently, tenderly, lovingly. 'And it took you leaving me for me to realise.' He took a shuddering breath. 'Oh, Kate, can you ever forgive me for letting you go?'

She couldn't answer, couldn't say what she was feeling—how suddenly she was coming back to life, how her blood was warm and vibrant in her veins, how the numb despair was flooding downwards through her limbs and back into the earth, washing away like a terrible, debilitating, nightmarish shadow.

His voice was rough and full of need and she reached up to return his kiss. 'I love you,

239

Ben,' she whispered.

'Do you?' He gazed at her, his face creased with lines of doubt. 'I didn't know. I wasn't sure. I thought you'd made your life up here. I thought I had to let you go.'

She shook her head. 'There hasn't been a moment I haven't thought of you. Or the boys. I love you all so much.'

'Then why didn't you tell me?' He hugged her against him. 'Oh, Kate. If only I'd known.'

She smothered a sob that rose inside her, desperate to be let out. 'Come home,' she whispered.

And then he laughed above her and she looked up. 'No,' he told her, his eyes gleaming with a silvery, joyful glitter. '*You* come home, my darling. Where you belong.'

*   *   *

They fell into each other's arms the moment they closed the door of her little cottage. Love came with a passion born of separation and discovery and a new-found fire that barely quenched the desire which filled them both. Words were unnecessary. Only words of love melded them together. Kate gave herself up to the exquisite joy and the release of fear and the knowledge that her life was changing without pain.

Later, they lay side by side, warm and content. Ben stretched lazily and turned on his side to stare at Kate, running a finger over her chin. As he lowered his head to kiss her and follow a breathless path over her naked shoulders, he sighed, running his fingers through her hair, which covered the pillow in golden rivers.

She turned toward him, blissfully at peace for the first time in months. 'How did you find me this morning?' she asked, suddenly curious.

He grinned. 'Called here first. Followed every damn path I could find around this village. I couldn't believe it when I saw you . . . I thought you were a mirage.'

She laughed. 'I never usually walk that way.'

'Then that's fate for you. I was meant to stumble across the woman I'd loved and lost, even though she'd taken the wrong turning.' He chuckled, pulling her towards him. 'Do you think I'm ever going to let you go again? After this?' He lifted her chin to gaze into her eyes. 'Kate, will you come home?'

She held her breath. 'Oh, Ben—'

'Don't answer me now. Not if it's no. You'd be taking on a lot—too much perhaps? I couldn't expect you to want a ready-made family, but I can't live without you. I was so afraid of loving again and yet now the thought of an existence without you is unbearable. And if it's children you want . . .'

'Is that your final offer?' She slid her arms around his neck.

'It's all I have.' He shuddered. 'Don't tease

me, Kate. I want it all with you. With the boys and with our own babies. As long as we're together I can face the future, whatever it holds.'

She hugged him and tears filled her eyes, but she wasn't going to cry again. She'd shed enough tears today for a hundred years.

'And before you answer, there's something else you should know,' he hurried on. 'I've a confession to make. That day when Julian arrived at the surgery? I was consumed with jealousy. Kate, it burned inside me. Shook me to the core. God, I didn't know what was happening to me. Can you love a man with such hopeless self-control?'

Kate found herself laughing. 'I felt it, too,' she admitted reluctantly. 'Every time I saw you with Mary Graham.'

'Mary?' He frowned. 'But, Kate, Mary's besotted with Damian. She's over the moon in love with the man.' He kissed the tip of her nose. 'I'd have thought the grapevine would have torn that one to pieces by now.'

'Damian?' Kate stared at him incredulously. 'I hadn't realised, no.'

'Then you should have asked me,' he said with a chuckle. 'Were you really very jealous?'

She nodded. 'Hopelessly.'

'Good.' He pulled her tightly against him. 'I'm glad you've suffered as much as I have.'

Kate thought he would never know how much, but she wasn't about to tell him now.

There would be other times, other places, other nights.

'Kate, there's no one else for me. Or the boys. They want you back as badly as I do.' His eyes met hers in a look of longing. 'We're all at a loss without you. Marry me, Kate. Come home and work with me. Let's build our future together.'

She was silent for a moment, unable to believe the words she was hearing. 'But you don't need another partner at the practice,' was all she could find to gasp.

'We will. Meg wants to retire. There's no one else in the world who could fill her place better than the woman in my arms.' He bent to whisper in her ear, his breath fanning warmly on her neck, 'Kate, will you—will you be my wife?'

In ecstasy, she closed her eyes. 'Yes, yes . . .'

He trapped her chin between his fingers, his eyes piercingly bright. 'You can't imagine what you mean to me . . .'

She lifted her mouth to his lips, smiling softly. 'Then show me, my darling. And don't leave anything to my imagination.'

APL		CCS	
Cen		Ear	
Mob		Cou	
ALL		Jub	
WH		CHE	
Ald		Bel	
Fin		Fol	
Can	4-2-1 R	STO	
Til		HCL	